Tales of a Persian Teenager

Mahshid Amirshahi

Translated from the Persian by J.E. Knörzer

Introduction by Hafez Farmayan

CENTER FOR MIDDLE EASTERN STUDIES
THE UNIVERSITY OF TEXAS AT AUSTIN

Library of Congress Catalogue Card Number: 95-067383

ISBN 0-292-70463-1

Printed in the United States of America

Cover: Diane Watts

Editor: Annes McCann-Baker

Distributed by arrangement with the University of Texas Press
Box 7819, Austin, Texas 78713

Contents

Introduction

This book of short stories is the first volume in English translation
that is dedicated entirely to the work of Mahshid Amirshahi. Previ-
ously, several short stories written by this significant Iranian author
had appeared in English in volume three of the journal *Edebiyat* (1978)
and *Stories from Iran: A Chicago Anthology, 1921-1991*, edited by Heshmat
Moayyad. This present volume contains eight works from those quaintly
referred to as "Suri Stories" by Iranian readers. Although related
thematically, these stories originally appeared in different collections
published between 1968 and 1971. Here, these "Suri Stories," appearing
together for the first time in one volume, give English readers an
opportunity to look at Amirshahi's short stories as a whole, from a
social perspective as well as that of style and content.

Mahshid Amirshahi was born into a wealthy upper-class family.
After primary and secondary education in Iran she was sent, like most
members of her class, to Europe to get a degree of higher education,
preferably by her family in some aspect of science and technology. This
she acceded to by attending the Woolwich Polytechnic of London
University where she received in 1963 a B.S. degree in physics. However, Amirshahi's personal interest was not science. As soon as she
returned to Iran in 1964, she plunged into a career of writing that
included numerous translations from English to Persian, non-fictional
essays which she contributed to literary journals, and editorship of a
children's book program. Among her various translations into Persian,
the most noteworthy are James Thurber's *Fables For Our Time*; E. B.
White's *Charlotte's Web*; Lawrence Durrell's *Alexandria Quartet*; and P.
L. Travers' *Mary Poppins*. Amirshahi's first collections of short stories
were published at intervals in Tehran in the 1960s and 1970s. These
were received enthusiastically by the general public and by writers and
literary critics. Due also to her attractive presence and outgoing person-
ality, she made many friends and, eventually, a circle formed around
her whose members included men and women of letters who repre-
sented the intellectual elite of Tehran society. She is perhaps the only
Iranian woman writer who has held regular literary gatherings at her
house for authors and artists and other interested members of the
Iranian elite.

By the time her first collection of short stories appeared in 1966,
Amirshahi had developed the style by which she was to make a name
for herself in the Iranian literary scene. This approach, which she still

uses, as in the case of her 1987 novel *Dar Hazar* (At Home), rests comfortably upon the classical Persian language in its purest form: clarity, directness, simplicity, the right usage of words, and correct syntax which results in solid, lucid sentences containing her own original stamp. She is not interested in creating special literary effects which too often result in dense cumbersome prose. She is interested in a form of writing that makes for easy reading. Her effort is to make her work understood by readers, rather than making readers conscious of unusual writing. The mixture of spoken and literary language makes her work somewhat reminiscent of that of the early twentieth-century Persian writer Mohammad Ali Jamalzadeh, or the American Ernest Hemingway.

Amirshahi's short stories, particularly those selected for this volume, depict the lives of the upper-middle-class Iranians who lived in the busy metropolis of Tehran between the 1950s and 1970s. This is the period in which the author grows from childhood to adulthood. It is also a dynamic and critical period in Iranian history. It is the apex of modernization in Iran. Modernization, which for all practical purposes could be called Westernization, was a process which began in the nineteenth century, but not until the early years of the 1920s did it begin to accelerate. At first this was a slow process, for Iran lacked both funds and technologies. However, by the late 1950s, certain crucial factors had quickened this process. The political upheavals of World War II and its aftermath led to the nationalization of the country's oil industry. Despite its unfortunate international political repercussions, once the oil crisis was resolved in 1953, gold began to flood Iran's treasury. State revenues from oil which in 1952 were essentially nil, in 1962 reached 323 million and by 1975 had soared to an annual 28.5 billion dollars.

The city of Tehran was the symbol of this amazing era which transpired. In many ways a golden period of increased prosperity and apparently solid achievement, it was shattered, finally, by its excesses and widespread lack of perception of the potential violence of the disparate social and economic forces which had been unleashed. Portions of population had embraced a totally Western way of life and other larger portions of it had become various mixtures of older tradition and modernity. In Tehran, most of the upper middle class lived in the northern part of the city. Its members patronized its fabulous hotels, shopping centers, restaurants and night clubs. They also consumed or patronized the quintessence of twentieth-century cultures worldwide, including that of Iran. This was a Western style of life quite different from that which existed in the south of Tehran. Mahshid Amirshahi grew up, lived and worked in north Tehran. Her success as a writer may be attributed to the fact that she can write confidently about her own class and its environment. More than any other Iranian writer of this period, she has been able to interpret in human terms the cataclysm which occurred in Iran in the latter 1960s and 1970s, brought about by the meeting of the East and the West. The stories that appear in *Suri & Co.* reflect to a certain extent the author's own life. One may surmise that Suri is a fictionally altered Mahshid. Whether it is the Suri collection or other stories, Amirshahi always works within her own milieu. This fact, along with her clever satire and her masterful dialogue writing, makes her a great rarity among modern Iranian writers. Her slashing wit delivers devastating blows at Iran's ruling class although she herself is part and parcel of that class. Extremely critical but not judgmental of the society which she describes, she does not hold a grudge against any particular segment of it. Many characters in her stories are men and women of depressed classes. Yet, she does not necessarily feel obliged to angrily defend their rights. Unlike many contemporary Iranian writers, her works do not reflect class warfare. She does not defend radicals against conservatives, poor against rich, people against government, peasants against landlords and so forth. In short, Amirshahi is not a wrathful author. An observer and sympathizer, her writings are humorous and rational.

After the Islamic Revolution of 1979, Amirshahi left Iran, perhaps permanently. Like many self-exiled writers, she has chosen to live in Paris. In 1987, she produced her first long work, a novel entitled *Dar Hazar* (At Home), which is about the coming of the Islamic Revolution and its immediate aftermath. At present she is completing her second novel *Dar Safar* (Away). After arriving in Paris, Amirshahi joined one of the Iranian opposition groups in exile and has become a political activist. It seems that now she has finally found a cause to join the growing ranks of rebellious Iranian writers.

The stories in the present volume are translated by Jutta Edith Knörzer who holds a Ph.D. degree in Persian and Islamic Studies from the University of Toronto. She has published several articles dealing with Persian literature. A book of hers is a scholarly study of the earlier twentieth-century Iranian writer, Ali Dashti, released by Mazda Publishers in 1994 under the auspices of the Persian Cultural Foundation (U.S.A.). The Middle East Center at The University of Texas is most pleased to present this talented scholar as translator of this collection of short stories by Mahshid Amirshahi.

Hafez Farmayan
Professor of History and Director of Iranian Studies
The University of Texas at Austin

Translator's Preface

Suri & Co.: Tales of a Persian Teenage Girl, by Mahshid Amirshahi, presents us with a refreshingly new perspective on Iranian life and society. Unlike the picture painted in most other modern Persian short fiction, *Suri & Co.* is neither gloomy nor violent nor peopled with (stereo)typical downtrodden, veiled females.[1] Instead, a high-spirited, intelligent, self-willed (though at times clumsy and insecure) teenager recounts, vignette-style, a number of highlights of her life in Iran over a period of fifteen years or so preceding the Islamic Revolution of 1979. Suri is certainly no female Iranian counterpart to the young David Copperfield: she is not a tyrannized teenager or an oppressed female in a men's world; rather, both in her inherent attitude and her behavior towards the adults around her, she resembles a Middle Eastern, upper middle-class version of Astrid Lindgren's *Pippi Longstocking* or L.M. Montgomery's *Anne of Green Gables*—albeit without Pippi's rebellious stance towards school and intellectual matters generally. Indeed, Suri reveals a strong bent to—of all things—mathematics and the sciences (in which she appears to resemble her creator).

Suri & Co. can be approached from various angles. These are stories of human interest and small-scale social comment, not political or ideological statements thinly disguised as literature. Perhaps the most salient literary device to strike the reader is the humor in these stories: at times deceptively simple, even simplistic slapstick, it is at other times psychologically very sophisticated and subtle, while also covering the entire range between these two extremes. This style of humor travels well and accomplishes that altogether rare feat of escaping from culture-bound, "ethnic" drollery.

Often, when rendering from one foreign language to another, from one ostensibly "exotic" culture to another, the translator or reader is confronted with the more or less incomprehensible. Generally, this is not the case with Amirshahi's writing. However, although the stories sometimes are—in almost cinematographic style—allusive and not fully explicit (for example, about family relationships between certain characters, especially where intermarriage is involved), there are layers of subtlety over and above the obvious which depend on Persian social and cultural interaction. One case in point may be the total lack of *ta'arof* (an elaborate system of etiquette in both manners and speech for traditional social occasions) or, on the contrary, the employment of an exaggerated form of *ta'arof* for humorous effect. (See end of Story 6.) Yet

1

other examples are the open offenses against Persian or Islamic conventions (e.g. Story 4: Suri not knowing how to wear a *chador* and giggling at the outward form of the mourning ritual; also Story 5, where Amir jokes about what might have been the baby's name if the Koran had opened at the wrong page.)

Perhaps more commonplace in the stories is the fact that a knowledge of Iranian historical and social events, e.g. the seizure of lands during the so-called White Revolution, is taken for granted. These stories were, after all, written for "domestic consumption," which is precisely what helps to make them more "authentic" and natural than some exile literature.

Despite a mainly "happy-family" atmosphere depicted in *Suri & Co.*, there are nonetheless subtle tensions and conflicts between men and women, adults and children or teenagers, and brothers and sisters. Suri is sent, under male escort, to the Karaj Archives to inspect a document merely because her elder brother (referred to as Dadash) is out of town (Story 2); in the (unexplained) absence of her natural father, the closest male relatives shape her life in the world outside the home, and even down to something as superficial as her hairdo. All this takes place according to a more-or-less rigid hierarchical code: Uncle Ardeshir, Dadash, her brother-in-law Amir, and so on. Thus, it would never occur to Mama to pick up the phone and arrange an interview for Suri with a government official when she wants to get a summer job: it would be highly unseemly, and Mama would most definitely not have the right connections to do so. Uncle Ardeshir jumps in with both feet, and makes a "fine mess" of it!

Portrayed with the same fine brush is the dichotomy between underlying Persian or Islamic *mores*[2] and only partly assimilated Western styles: there is a pseudo-fundamentalist official who pronounces Persian as if it were Arabic, grating to many Iranian ears not only linguistically but also because of its association with a pompous cleric's speech; smoking opium is acceptable for a man, smoking cigarettes for a teenager or young woman is not. (Story 2) Since the stories are set in an Iran, years before the Islamic Revolution, when at least some of the urban, middle-to-upper-class young were still in thrall to *gharbzadegi*,[3] the teenagers attach a certain cachet to speaking English among themselves—however inadequate or badly accented it may be. (Story 3)

In the style of *Suri & Co.*, it will be noticed that Suri often speaks to an unspecified "you." This may indicate that the stories are part of a diary; or letters to a friend; or addressed, Victorian-style, to the "Gentle

Reader." The language of *Suri & Co.* is normally unforced colloquial in the narrative, with appropriate variations to fit each speaker. In virtually no instance does it degenerate into extreme slang, jargon, or obscenity as with several recent (pre-Revolutionary), would-be realistic writers. Very short sentences are the norm, but this aspect has not always been reproduced where it would conflict with the expectations of an English reader. Nor have the heavily repeated, and quite monotonous, occurrences of *goft* ("he/she said") to introduce each item of dialogue been translated literally: where possible they have been omitted, elsewhere other expressions have been introduced.

One supposes that a certain amount of autobiographical material is to be found in these stories. Waxing lyrical and nostalgic about Tehran's changed skyline and street-names (Story 8) seems not a typical teenage preoccupation and may, of course, even imply discreet criticism by the author of the social and architectural modernization drive under the Pahlavi rulers.

* * *

The stories published here were selected by the author herself in consultation with Professor Hafez F. Farmayan, of the University of Texas. They first appeared in Persian in the following three collections: *Sar-e Bibi Khanom*, 1347/1968; *Ba'd az ruz-e akher*, 1348/1969; and *Beh sigheh-e avval-e shakhs-e mofrad*, 1350/1971.

I am deeply grateful to Professor Farmayan for suggesting my name to translate these stories, for his introduction to the book, and for his encouraging support of the project as a whole. He also advised me about certain social, cultural, and linguistic nuances, to which only an "insider" like himself would have natural access.

I also owe thanks to Professor G.M. Wickens, University Professor Emeritus at Toronto and himself an experienced translator of literary texts, for taking the time to read through my versions and make many valuable suggestions.

Any shortcomings are my own responsibility.

J.E.Knörzer
Toronto
Spring 1995

[1] See, for example, the anthologies by Soraya Paknazar Sullivan (tr.), *Stories by Iranian Women Since the Revolution* (Austin, 1991) and Minoo Southgate (ed./ tr.), *Modern Persian Short Stories* (Washington, D.C., 1980). Compare these, however, with *Stories from Iran: A Chicago Anthology, 1921-1991*, ed. by Heshmat Moayyad (Washington, D.C., 1991).

[2] Of course, Europeans and North Americans have, for long, erroneously equated Persian with Islamic culture or assumed that Persian is a dialect of Arabic.

[3] Literally "west-struckness," a pejorative term for uncritical enthusiasm over every aspect of Western life and culture. The admiration tended in fact to be given to the most materialistic and permissive features.

Principal Characters

Ali Aqa:
General factotum and chauffeur in Suri's family, and a particular friend of hers.

Amir:
Husband of Suri's sister Simin. Something of an insensitive smart aleck.

Ardeshir:
See Uncle Ardeshir.

Auntie Fakhri:
A relative of Suri's with few redeeming features: greedy, hypocritical, shallow, vain, and interfering.

Big Brother:
See Dadash.

Dadash:
Suri's only and "elder brother" (this is the meaning of the semi-colloquial term *Dadash*), who constantly tries to boss her around. He is rarely successful in this, and is no match for her in intelligence and repartee. Married to Maliheh. His personal name is Sasan.

Fakhri:
See Auntie Fakhri.

Firuz:
A young man on whom Suri had a youthful crush, but who disappoints her when, on his return from studying abroad, he displays various ludicrous Western affectations.

Khanom Jan:
An undesignated relative, or perhaps just a close friend of the family. This elderly lady has a soft spot for Suri and vice versa. Indeed, Suri regards her as a great fount of practical wisdom and a diplomatic intermediary in family crises.

Maliheh:
> Dadash's wife and Suri's sister-in-law. Basically a well-meaning person, with idealistic views on women's rights.

Mama:
> Suri's mother. A woman of some simplicity but with practical good sense, who deals fairly effectively with her family of three children—Dadash, Simin, and the *enfant terrible* Suri herself. At the same time, she tends to rely, in matters of the wider world, on the not always sound guidance of Uncle Ardeshir.

Mansur Khan:
> An undefined male relative or friend of the family. Suri is constantly turned off by his froglike appearance and vaguely lecherous manner.

Mehri:
> Suri's best friend. She is very dependent on Suri, particularly for help in school work, and their relationship vacillates between close affection and a marked coolness.

Simin:
> Suri's elder sister, a somewhat feeble character who appears very much in the shadow of her husband Amir.

Suri:
> The first-person narrator of the stories, all of which revolve around her own experiences with her family and others she meets through them. She is a turbulent, but highly intelligent teenager (her age is given clearly in only one story—"The Interview"—as 16+, though elsewhere she may be a year or two younger). Her observations are trenchant, even harsh, and sometimes obviously exaggerated, but they form a valid and amusing commentary on Persian family life in particular and the human condition in general. She tends to look down upon her less-bright contemporaries and on most of her elders.

Uncle Ardeshir:
> In the apparent absence of Suri's father, this character serves as her most authoritative male relative. Educated at the American

College in Tehran and a minor British private school, he is shown as aping British manners, dress, and speech so as to seem at times like a caricature of a testy, pompous British colonel. He is always clashing with Suri (who often treats him as something of an incompetent fool), but he is fundamentally kind towards her and even tactfully helpful in embarrassing situations.

NOTE:

There are several minor figures whose role or character is made sufficiently clear in the relevant story or stories. These comprise relatives, family- and school-friends, public officials, servants, etc.

Suri & Co.

Tales of a Persian Teenager

Big Brother's Future In-Laws[*]

I really wanted orange juice but was afraid that if I were to say "orange juice," everybody would consider me chicken. So I said, "whiskey."

Big Brother's eyebrows rose to just below his hairline. I was afraid that while the waiter was still at the table, my brother's amazement would reach the point where he would give my ear a hearty smack. One never knows how one stands with this guy Dadash. Two or three weeks earlier when we had gone out with Homa and Homayun and Auntie, Homa and Auntie had asked for coffee, Homayun and Dadash had wanted beer, and I had ordered cookies with a glass of cold milk. At that, Dadash said, "And bring it for her in a baby-bottle!"

The worst part was that on that day Mehri was sitting with a couple of her friends at the next table.

At school, Mehri wouldn't even take a sip of water without my permission. If I say today such-and-such a book is great, by tomorrow it will already be under her arm and she will tell everyone she meets what a fine book it is. And, if I were to curse Hafez and Sa'di,[**] Mehri would curse them, too: that's the extent of the faith she has in me. On that occasion, however, my big brother made me look worthless in front of Mehri; so, right until the day before the algebra exam, Mehri would not show me proper respect.

It's no good if I drink milk, and it's no good if I drink whiskey. Really, one doesn't know how one stands with this guy Dadash.

I looked at Simin to gather moral strength and saw that she was biting her lips and looking down. Thank God that Simin's husband hadn't come that day. He always looks on me as if I were a runty kid and introduces me to everyone as "a bit of bread under my meat"[***]— meaning "what does she amount to, after all?" Whenever I say something sensible—I *always* say sensible things, although nobody listens— he will say: "Ugh, God bless us!" By which he implies, "what booboos"

---

[*] Also translated by Michael Beard in the Chicago anthology referred to above, under the title "Brother's Future Family."

[**] Two of Iran's greatest classical poets, from the 13th and 14th centuries.

[***] Professor Farmayan informs me that this is a pejorative term for "sister-in-law."

11

or "what a lot of idle chatter!" He has forgotten that when Simin became engaged to him, she was only two years older than I am now.

If he were here, he would make me look thoroughly foolish. I didn't look at the others, only from the corner of my eye did I see a ridiculous laugh on Mansur Khan's face. Like the laugh of a person who's heard a good joke. As if Mansur Khan had a right to laugh like that! Mansur Khan, the guy who would squeeze my fingers so hard whenever we shook hands that his bulging eyes would get bloodshot, the guy who held my hand so long in his that it would get all sweaty—yuck! And he looks at me in a way he has no right to do...I'll give him something in return that he will really enjoy. If I cared enough about him, I would.

The only person who took me seriously was the waiter. He asked, "With ice and soda?"

I replied, "Yes."

My uncle Ardeshir who considers himself an expert on all things, great and small—why? Because in his younger days he had spent six or seven months in some crummy British school—said: "Whiskey spoils one's day."

I didn't answer him.

Maliheh asked, "How long have you been a whiskey-drinker!?"

I answered, "Sure, a long time." And I waved my hand in the air. If only I could stop waving my hand—I was overdoing it. I suppose I was trying to say that I'd always drunk whiskey instead of milk. Everybody began to snigger except Dadash, who was eying me narrowly, and Maliheh's father who didn't look at me at all. Maliheh's father kept his eyes fixed on the food and looked at it with such concentration, that it might've been the climax of a thriller, right on the page where the identity of the killer is revealed. Worse than all was Maliheh's mother. She gave me such a look that I just about turned into a cockroach climbing the wall.

I should've asked for that orange-juice. Especially since everybody here considered me just a young chick anyway, and whiskey makes matters worse rather than better—but it was now too late, and I thought, "Come what may, I'll have to stick it out now to the bitter end."

The waiter brought the whiskey and placed it before me. Brother dear was fidgeting on his chair, and I thought he was about to take the glass away from me. So I quickly picked it up myself and—glug! glug!—gulped it down like a lemonade.

Since I knew that they were all looking at me, I suppressed my cough no matter what and even managed something of a smile.

My eyes fell on the mirror behind Simin. I saw that I had become like one of those masks, simultaneously crying and laughing, which are hung over the doors of theaters: I was not like either of them individually, but like both combined.

Dadash said softly and angrily: "You've really wasted good stuff. If you have to drink whiskey, at least drink it like a man!" He spoke so softly that—what can I say?—not only our table but literally everybody in the restaurant heard it.

Sure enough! My brother thinks I'm still a five-year old kid and that he has to teach me everything. Everybody had heard Dadash's instructions, he thinks of himself as the leading whiskey-drinker! O.K., so I don't know how to drink whiskey. But it isn't only whiskey. Brother thinks I know nothing about anything. For example, he thinks that I didn't realize that a few days ago he was busily engaged smooching with Maliheh under the trees at the far end of the garden. By the time I arrived Maliheh had drawn away and Dadash had begun to whistle. I could easily have gone to Mama and told her, so that she would give him hell. But I didn't. Even to Dadash himself I didn't let on that I realized what was going on. My fault. If I had explained to him that I had seen and understood everything, he would never have made such a fuss over a lousy glass of whiskey in front of all these people. Especially in front of this sleazy Mansur Khan with his crafty smirk! Those bulging eyes! What a disaster!

My eye fell once again on the mirror behind Simin: the tip of my nose was shiny and I had gone beet-red. In the words of Mama, I looked "a right mess." Until then I had not understood properly what "a right mess" looked like. At that moment I was sure that the "right mess" must be me in the mirror behind Simin's head. My head was starting to spin.

I said, "Kids …"

Dadash yelped, "*Kids* !? Shut your mouth! Who you talking to? Look at the little squirt!"

I pretended not to hear his remarks but said: "Kids, do you know what 'a right mess' looks like?"

I really don't know why I fixed my eyes on Maliheh's daddy. He was giving me a black look and I realized that he too might fit the picture. I was scared that he might be able to read my thoughts and said, "I didn't mean you."

Simin got all steamed up to say something, but the waiter brought the food and I was saved from her attack.

A piece of meat was positively squealing in the middle of the plate and looking at me. Even worse than my meat was Mansur Khan's fish—I was certain that it was squirming. The knives and forks began to be wielded as if to cut up the flesh of my body. The noise of the knives and forks was like the sound of chalk being scraped across a blackboard. It sent shivers down my spine. I was afraid that if I looked at my plate, I'd throw up all over the table. I spread the napkin over my plate. But it was a paper napkin, and the juice and blood of the meat and the slimy greenness of the beans and peas made a pattern on it. The outline of the food became visible once more, only this time it was as if someone had slobbered all over it. I was very close to puking. Bad as things were, however, I pulled myself together.

All at once, Simin said across the table, "Aren't you eating?"

If this nosy dame hadn't said anything, Dadash wouldn't have noticed. But as soon as Simin said, "Aren't you eating?", he gave up his confidential whispering to Maliheh and said abruptly, angrily: "Why aren't you eating?!"

"I can't," I replied. I was afraid he might force me and was close to crying.

Maliheh realized I was telling the truth and that I couldn't eat. She asked Dadash: "Why are you always down on her? So what if she can't eat?"

Maliheh is basically a decent girl. In order to show that I knew she was a decent girl, I said: "Maliheh, I know that what happened the day before yesterday under the trees was all Dadash's fault."

I knew that Big Brother would be annoyed about what I had said— but not that he would react so violently. Suddenly, he half got up from his chair and said: "If you don't hold your tongue, you'll get a thorough thrashing tonight." And his eyes protruded so much from their sockets that I thought they would plop out onto the plate, and that if I didn't stop him real quickly, I'd get a whacking right here at the table.

I said to him, "I haven't told Mama yet, but if you kick up too much dust I *will* tell her what you and Maliheh were up to."

Maliheh's mother raised her eyebrows and asked, "What was that, dearie? What did you say, dearie?"

Maliheh's mother calls everyone "dearie" and her eyebrows are always up in the air. That's why my mother calls her "Mrs. Hifalutin."

I said, "I wasn't addressing you, Mrs. Hifalutin." She asked, "Mrs. Whaaat? God bless you."

Maliheh's mother is always "God blessing" everybody.

I replied: "Mrs. Hifalutin. My mama calls you Mrs. Hifalutin. Do you know why ...?"

Once more Dadash blew his top and shouted so loudly that Maliheh's daddy got alarmed and dropped his fork.

My brother leaned across the table and briskly wiped the collar and shirt-front of Maliheh's father, calling out to the waiter: "Bring a fork for this gentleman. Right away."

"Bring him a pair of trousers, too," I added. "That's more urgent."

Maliheh's mama: "Very well. Thanks a lot. Now, what else, dearie?"

I replied, "Nothing more, dearie. God bless you." And my voice sounded so much like that of Maliheh's mama that I almost died laughing. However, nobody else was laughing, and I couldn't go on laughing all alone.

Everything was moving ahead in double-quick time, like the films of Charlie Chaplin. People's words likewise, like a 33-rpm record being played at 78-rpm speed.

I caught sight of Maliheh and noticed she looked upset. I felt sorry for her. I was near to tears myself and said to her, "Maliheh, dear…"

However, she wasn't having any of this. In fact, she shot back at me, "Damn you, and your 'Maliheh, dear!'"

I tried another tack: "Look here, Maliheh, that day under the trees—it was all…"

But you think they'd let me finish? From one end of the table Maliheh's father gave a snort, and from the other end her mother uttered one of those pious cries of hers that made you think she'd fainted clean away. Even Simin kept exclaiming bitterly, "Ugh, what a scandal! Ugh, what a disgrace!"

I asked her, "What's the matter, Simin dear? You yourself never liked this bunch…"

"That'll do," she replied.

But I insisted: "I'll say this much and no more. Have you forgotten that day when Mama said 'Dadash has finally started to mess around with this girl, so now he'll have to marry her…'? Remember what you said? *Remember* ?!"

Absolute silence…

"You said 'There's a girl really dying for Big Brother to…'"

At this point Maliheh cried out aloud, "Mama, let's get up and leave!"

Maliheh's mother picked up her gloves and purse and turned to Big Brother: "Look here, dearie! Maliheh isn't right for you, dearie. Actually, we aren't right for you at all, dearie. I'm Mrs. Whatsername and my husband's got a crooked nose." (Nobody had in fact said that her husband's nose was crooked, but in the case of Maliheh's mother, if she herself has one fault, she has to heap a hundred others on her husband's head, to stay one-up on him.) And she went on: "In addition, there're 1001 other things you have against us, but to prevent you laying further faults and defects at our door—may God bless you!—we'll get going."

Dadash wailed, "Dear madam, the things that were said…"

"You can keep your 'dear madam,' son. Bless you. One remark came from your mother, the other from your sister, dearie." With these words she pointed at me, from top to toe, with her gloves to indicate that she didn't mean Simin.

All three stood up together and left without even saying good-bye. Immediately, Simin followed them in great haste. Big Brother now launched an attack on me, but Uncle Ardeshir seized his arm and said, "Sit down again. Don't create any further scandal right here in the restaurant."

Sometimes Uncle Ardeshir hits the nail on the head. Dadash resumed his seat, but continued to glare at me like a watch dog on the alert.

When we rose from the table, I didn't know whether I was weightless or terribly heavy. To put it simply, I couldn't walk properly. I even took Uncle Ardeshir's arm so as not to fall. He suggested, "Let's go and have coffee somewhere, and help this girl get over it."

"Coffee?!" asked Mansur Khan, and he said it in such a way as to imply that coffee was some sort of precious jewel, hard to obtain—or even if it could be obtained, it was not something one should drink. Finally, if it *were* something to drink, it would not help my present condition, anyway.

I muttered under my breath, "Ugh! Get lost, you slimy frog!"

He countered, "How's that again?!"

I was in quite a state once more. I pulled my head down into my collar and popped my eyes in an attempt to look like Mansur Khan, and said: "Yes, and much worse. You randy little squirt, you! Randy and all the other things you are."

Mansur Khan's eyes bulged even more and his cowlick started to quiver: "Impudence! Shameless hussy!" With each word his voice became more shrill. It reminded me of the hackneyed insults one hears in corny radio shows. I was dying with laughter, but I restrained myself and placed my hand on my heart, "Oh, my dear man!" However,

Mansur Khan didn't wait for my laughter nor for my little piece of theatrics. Instead, he immediately sidled out of the restaurant, moving like a crab.

Big Brother grabbed my arm and squeezed it so hard that I cried out, "What's wrong with you?! You're breaking my arm, you dummy!"

"Stop shouting!" he shot back. "You stupid girl. If I could, I'd break your neck."

"When did *I* shout?"

"Shut up for a minute, or I'll give you one in the mouth and knock your teeth down your throat!"

I noticed the people at the other tables were all looking at us. I asked the gentleman sitting closest to us, who was wearing two ties and two pairs of glasses: "This is what they call Big Brother. What would *you* call him?" Then I realized that both this gentleman's ties were crooked, so I took a step in his direction intending to straighten them out. Uncle Ardeshir dragged me away and took me outside.

Big Brother still had to make his comment: "I'll do you a real good turn, my girl. You just wait!"

I answered him back: "So what dumb thing are you going to do now?" At that moment I wasn't afraid of Big Brother, nor did I give a hang what might happen later.

When my head cleared a bit, it hit me what a booboo I had made. Of course, Big Brother did keep his promise—to do me a real good turn—and for a whole month he gave me a terribly hard time and barely allowed me to take one quiet breath. He was constantly bugging me and threatening to tell Mama the whole story.

∞　∞　∞

On another occasion, when I was only seven or eight, he had harassed me in the same way. That was because I had dropped an expensive fancy comb of mine down the toilet. Dadash, who is never able to contain himself, came into the john while I was still there and immediately took in the situation. Of course, I hadn't deliberately thrown my comb in, it had fallen out of my hair. Anyway, I did a stupid thing and promptly flushed the toilet. The comb wouldn't go down. When Big Brother came in, I was pulling the plug for the third time, and he arrived just at the right moment to see what had happened. For quite a while after that he never gave me a quiet moment.

For two or three weeks I was nothing but his servant-girl, just so that he shouldn't tell Mama. For example, he would yell at me to bring him a drink of water, or sometimes get me to tie his shoelaces. He would tell me to tidy up his clothes-closet. As for the two or three days when the contractor and his workmen were there trying to unblock the toilet—let's not even talk about that! I was practically skinned alive.

One day he addressed me so roughly that Mama got real upset. She shouted at him: "Why do you keep ordering a little child around in this way?"

Dadash replied, "She herself knows. She has to do everything I say. Otherwise…"

Like lightning I jumped up to obey his instructions, but Mama said, "Hold it right there! I intend to find out why this fat bully won't do his own chores."

Big Brother looked at me out of the corner of his eye. "I'll tell on you, see if I don't!"

I was in a terrible state. Mama then asked, "What on earth are you talking about?"

He now told the whole story, from beginning to end.

Mama's reaction was, "Is that all? O.K., so she dropped it in there. For a worthless comb you tormented that poor child like that?" Then she turned to me: "My dear, if you'd only told me yourself at the time, I'd have asked someone to get it out so that the toilet-pipe wouldn't get blocked."

I felt exactly as though a mountain had been lifted from my shoulders. Dadash, on the other hand, was totally deflated.

∞   ∞   ∞

On this present occasion too, I several times thought of throwing caution to the winds and telling Mama the whole story.

But this predicament was an altogether different one. In short, for a whole month—in fact right up to the evening of the engagement of Dadash and Maliheh—he gave me absolute hell.

On that evening Maliheh's mother went around showering so many cries of "God bless you!" on me that you'd have thought I had never uttered those offending words. She held my arm and introduced me formally to everyone as they arrived. I might myself have been the new bride in the family. Satan was whispering to me to have another go at the whiskey, but you can bet she wouldn't allow me to stir from her side. So I had a good slug of orange juice. It can't be denied, it tastes much nicer than whiskey.

On the other hand, next day I said to Mehri, "Last night was Big Brother's engagement party. You should've been there, we really hit the whiskey."

That was the evening when Mehri decided to try whiskey for herself.

My Grandfather, the Grandson
of this Gentleman's Mother's Aunt!

I can never get away from this one or that one. Whoever you can imagine, he will be lording it over me. I thought that when Big Brother and Maliheh had moved to a place of their own, I would be breathing easy—some free breathing! God help us! The whole gang of them have turned against me, and they won't let up. Wherever you turn, spikes poke into your feet as plentiful as weeds. They all tell you what to do and they all want to bring you up nicely. Their empty talk makes one sick, it reminds one of the lessons in grade school: Behave properly, so that you grow up properly! Get up early in the morning, so that you may be successful! And similar nonsense...Really, one's stomach turns.

Anyway, what I really wanted to say was that one day I went with Uncle Ardeshir to the Registry Office at Karaj in order to inspect a file. Actually, I had no idea what it was all about. Mama had put into my hand a piece of paper that was like an incantation of the fortune-tellers, a mixture of numbers, letters, diagrams, and pictures and told me: "You're going to the Registry with your uncle. You're going to get this file and read it properly. Read it and see which bits are mortgaged and which ones are not, and then write it down on a piece of paper."

Uncle asked Mama, "Do you think she'll be able to understand it?"

If you please! That's a really good start! No, I can't understand it! Uncle Ardeshir thinks apart from himself nobody knows anything. I was livid.

I said, "Mom, for God's sake, *say* something to this uncle. I *do* know how to read and write. Hang it all, this year I'm gonna graduate from high school after all."

"Uncle is right, my girl. Understanding bureaucratic style isn't so easy."

I said: "It must be written in Chinese! I guess Uncle Ardeshir knows Chinese as well. But perhaps not."

Uncle Ardeshir, who is never put down, said: "No, I don't know Chinese. I know English and Latin." For every one thing Uncle Ardeshir does *not* know, he—God bless him!—knows two others.

Mama turned to me: "Speak politely to your uncle and don't be difficult. If your brother were in Tehran, he would go himself and we'd be spared your cheeky remarks."

Here we go again! They don't treat me as a full human being. Because Brother is away...if he weren't on a trip, it would never enter their heads that I exist or that I can do things. I didn't particularly insist on doing a stupid job like this; it's only that if I didn't go, the chance of not going to school for a whole morning would be wasted.

On the road there Uncle Ardeshir asked: "Well, then. You're going there—what're you going to say?"

I didn't have the patience to play Question-and-Answer with Uncle Ardeshir. "Nothing. I'll just say that I want to see this file."

After eighteen years of driving, Uncle Ardeshir still stares in all directions when he is at the wheel. Anyone looking at him from outside the car must think he is doing the frog's breast-stroke. So, when he was talking to me, he was watching the road, not looking at me, and so didn't see when I said, "This file" while pointing to the fortune-teller's incantation.

"Which file?" he asked.

It was as if he wanted to catch me out. I held the piece of paper under his nose saying, "This file!" The tip of the paper brushed against his mouth.

Extra movements always upset Uncle's driving. The car swerved left, then right and I called out: "Watch it! We're going to hit the truck in front!" Things almost got exciting, but we didn't have a collision, just a taxi-driver threw a couple of filthy swear words at Uncle.

All the trouble they had taken over Uncle Ardeshir in England went down the drain. First, he answered back at the cab driver and then he turned angrily on me: "First thing is, take your hand away. Second, this...! I want this file!" He even imitated my voice, "Eh...eh...eh!" Really, the Big Cheese! But when Uncle Ardeshir drives, he is such a sad little creature that one doesn't dare confront him. Very calmly I asked: "So, what will I say?"

"Do you think it's that easy?"

Ugh! He was making me *tired*. There was no one to tell this Uncle, "Hey, man! When this girl asks you what she should do, speak up and don't fool around." I looked at his hands gripping the steering wheel, so that I might feel sorry for him and not get mad at him.

I said, "I did think it was that easy. What do *you* think I should do?"

He answered like some philosopher, "In matters like this, one must be diplomatic, my dear."

Ahem! Here was another precept to add to the list: Be diplomatic in order to succeed!

21

I sought a clarification, "How so, Uncle?"

He, in a mysterious tone, "We must find the right man for it—the man who can fix it properly."

You'd have thought I was wanting to do a bit of spying or stealing. Once again, my fury boiled up.

"Fix what, Uncle Ardeshir? I don't want to fix anything. I want to get hold of this file or deed or whatever, which concerns me and Brother and Mama—and then read it. Is this something illegal? Just to read it and then give it back to them. This doesn't need any great artistry."

One shouldn't answer Uncle back, because he goes off like a firecracker. He snapped back angrily, "Who're you going to ask for the file? Who? That doorman by the gate?!"

I replied coolly (which annoyed him): "No, Uncle dear. I'll go inside and ask somebody."

"Who? Some attendant or other?"

My patience gave out. "No, man! I'll ask whichever donkey looks after the files."

At this, he flared up: "Good grief!" He had forgotten what he'd said to the taxi driver and what he'd heard from him. I had simply said "donkey" and I got remarks like "Good grief!"

Anyway, here was the lesson: Behave yourself or you'll get one in the mouth!

"Sorry! I'll ask the gentleman who looks after the files." I never even thought of the phrase "stinking archivist," and I swallowed my anger.

As though he had scored a triumph, Uncle said, "Terrific! He's the very person you mustn't ask files from."

If there is one person in the world who *doesn't* get hot under the collar with Uncle Ardeshir, I'll be a monkey's uncle!

I asked, "All right then, why?"

If there is one day on which Uncle doesn't assert several times that he knows more than everyone else, it's a day lost. And now he was at it again. But to tell the truth, I was gradually losing heart. I thought, "God forbid! We're going to do this the wrong way."

I asked, "So, who shall I approach?"

Uncle cleared his throat and said in a fatherly way, "Yes, my dear. Ask so that you may learn. Never think you know all the answers."

Another lesson: In asking is a pleasure which is not to be found in answering. And again, who's the one giving this lesson? Uncle Ardeshir who considers himself the be-all and end-all of knowledge. And one isn't supposed to get furious?

I replied nothing and waited to see eventually who I should ask for the file.

Finally, Uncle Ardeshir came up with, "We'll go to the man at the top."

I'm always afraid of the "man at the top." Anyway, unlike me Uncle Ardeshir's business cannot be conducted without a man at the top. He even buys his cigarettes from the top tobacconist! His local sweeper has to be the top sweeper. I was too scared to speak.

Uncle, pleased at having given me a hard time, now played his trump card: "The top man is a relative of yours, my girl."

(I forgot to say that all the top men have some connection to Uncle.)

"What relation of mine is he?" I asked.

"Your late grandfather used to be the grandson of the paternal aunt of this gentleman's mother."

Now let's solve this problem with six x's. My grandfather...

"What?!" I almost passed out. "O.K., tell me: he must be seven times removed. He's certainly never seen me and he won't know me. How is he different from a stranger?"

Uncle rejoined, "In the first place, he knows *me*. Secondly, he knows you too. Don't you remember two brothers—Mahmud Khan and Ahmad Khan—used to come see your grandfather?"

Uncle Ardeshir has no great regard for my grandfather. What he was doing was reminding me how I should speak about my elders. When he lectures me like this, I only get more annoyed.

He persisted, "Don't you remember?"

I remembered all right. Two brothers, very similar in appearance, and both opium-smokers, the very caricature of addicts as drawn in cartoons. Their cheeks deeply hollow, their noses just a ridge of bone, their eyelids puffy and heavy, their lips a violet color, their necks sunken in their collars, listless and lifeless. I don't know why there came into my mind a sort of link between them and a cow or a sheep or a horse.

Uncle stopped the car two meters away from the curb. God forgive his father again! He usually tips it in the ditch.

I tried another tack in the hope of diverting Uncle from going to the top man. It didn't work. He said, "When will you ever learn how to handle affairs properly?"

And do you think it's just Uncle Ardeshir who wants to teach me "how to handle affairs properly?" Just watch how the top man also took me to task (remember: my grandfather had been the grandson of the paternal aunt of his mother).

First, let me speak of his appearance: he hadn't changed the least bit, nor had he grown older. The only thing was, until Uncle addressed him, I didn't know whether he was Ahmad Khan or Mahmud Khan. Grandad used to call them "Mahmud Khan the Elder" and "Ahmad Khan the Younger." Aha! Now the connection between these brothers and a horse was clear.*

Uncle Ardeshir greeted him fulsomely and asked, "Mahmud Khan, you know us of course?"

Mahmud Khan the Elder fixed his bleary eyes on me, but his glance passed through me to bounce off the wall behind me. Through his nose and with a voice like a young goat, he said, "Ye-e-es, ye-e-es."

Just think what a production it all was, with Uncle Ardeshir realizing that the fellow was talking nonsense and didn't know me at all, so he introduced me.

Mahmud Khan said, "I know her, I know her, I know her well. Hey boy, bring tea!" He wasn't able to raise and lower his voice, so that the latter phrase was on the same level as the words "I know her."

I said, "I don't drink tea, thank you. I came to…"

"What do you mean 'thank you?' Don't be difficult! Come over here and sit near me. Boy, bring the tea!"

Since Mahmud Khan the Elder was a century old, I wasn't allowed *not* to want tea. I took my seat and stopped being difficult.

If I say "I don't drink tea," it's rudeness and I'm being difficult. But when Mahmud Khan talks utter nonsense and weaves all sorts of fancies for three quarters of an hour (not even once asking what I'm here for), it's not rude and it's not being a nuisance. Uncle Ardeshir behaved as though I wasn't even in the room or as if we had absolutely no business to do there, and paid Mahmud Khan the closest attention.

You can't imagine how my patience finally gave out. If only you could see my nods and winks to Uncle behind Mahmud Khan's back! He saw them, but I realized it was no good. They were still busy talking about such characters as Zakiyeh Khanom and Mahram and Zolmat ol-Hajiyeh, and even if I were to cower in the corner like a poor orphan till tomorrow morning, it was clear they'd pay me no attention. I got out my cigarette case and lit up. I was certain that if I spoke out of the clouds of

---

* In Persian the word for "elder" (*mehtar*) also means "groom," "stable-boy."

24

smoke, Mahmud Khan would be intimidated and immediately look into my enquiry. But before I got my cigarette going properly, he turned his bent, twisted face in my direction and asked, "You mean to say you *smoke* ?!"

Yuck! What a bad moment for him to turn his head. My cigarette wasn't yet properly lit and I was killing myself to get it going. My hand was trembling too. My act was totally misplaced. I hung my head and made a few superfluous movements: I opened and shut my purse for no good reason, smoothed out my skirt, and tapped my cigarette (which still had no ash on the end) two or three times on the edge of the ashtray. These characters are out for one thing only—to make a person more confused than ever.

Anyway, he wouldn't let go, but pursed his violet-colored lips and banged his pen on the edge of his desk a few times (as though it were his tweezers holding the opium on his brazier), and said, "I can't believe my eyes!"

None of the things they did counted as bad behavior. It was all fatherly affection. I said to myself, "Believe your eyes, my foot!" But it's a fine thing when someone can't sit down and pluck up the courage to look this old junky in the eye and say, "Yes, I do smoke. Look all you want!" I blew hard into my handkerchief but it made a dry, ridiculous sound that made me cringe with embarrassment. I pushed my hair behind my ears and shifted from one foot to another. Mahmud Khan the Elder was now reproving me with silence and a fixed stare. But you know what made me mad? He was succeeding! I also wanted to cry out loud at the behavior of Uncle Ardeshir. Usually his mouth is always gaping like the top of a sack and he makes a display of his pearly whites. But now he'd been struck dumb, not saying one word to change the situation.

I made a movement to put my cigarette case back in my purse, hoping the matter would be forgotten. But Mahmud Khan, addict though he was, shot up and struck me so sharply on the hand that I didn't know whether I was coming or going. Then he picked up my case and put it in his own pocket. It was brand new, and I had wheedled it out of Mama the previous week and had been showing it off to Mehri at school. However, I had never found a suitable opportunity to smoke a single one of its contents, and now that the best possible chance had arisen, Mahmud Khan the Elder had spoiled it for me.

Thank God! Just when I was about to burst into tears, someone came into the room and saved me from the vicious looks of Mahmud

25

Khan's bleary eyes (to say nothing of the glances Uncle Ardeshir was giving me).

Mahmud Khan half got up from behind his desk and his prayer beads knocked over my glass of tea. Of course, Mahmud Khan being at least a hundred years old does *not* have to say, "I'm sorry."

I realized then that all these maxims had one corollary: Behave yourself until you're grown up, and then do whatever you want.

Anyway, Mahmud Khan and the new arrival were by now deep in conversation. My patience was totally exhausted. I picked up a file near my hand and started reading it for interest.

Item of Conveyance of Gift : All claims presumptive and conceivable, peremptory and irreplaceable, of the donor relating to the right of concession...pertaining thereto, whatever it may be, in a manner that shall not have been otherwise, on behalf of the donor by right or claim or variation of the donee in any aspect or regard, the legal and official representative of the donor who shall proceed in accordance with the provisions for the settlement of the interests involved...

Howzat? I had spots before my eyes. I read it once more, carefully:

Item of Conveyance of Gift :
....
for the settlement of the interests involved.

I didn't understand a single word. It was Chinese all right. Uncle Ardeshir had got that one right. But I badly wanted to know how much of it he himself would understand.

I closed the file and furtively put it back on the table. I prayed God that Uncle would not notice, because I was afraid he'd remember our own business. And to avoid Mahmud Khan rapping me on the hand again, I quickly took it away.

I now paid close attention to Mahmud Khan's pal. A real fossil in the fullest sense of the word. You should've seen him. He was wearing round glasses, and under one lense he had stuffed a dirty piece of cotton. His face was covered in spots, some coffee-colored, others milky. You'd have thought the skin had been scraped off his face and a sausage casing pulled over his skull in its place, with openings for eyes and nose and mouth. In short, Mahmud Khan, beside him, was an absolute Prince Charming. He smoked his cigarette like an old-fashioned pipe. I had a renewed craving for my cigarette.

No, Mahmud Khan obviously had no intention of asking my business. Truth to tell, I no longer wanted to see the file, but anyhow he should've asked why the devil I'd come here. Anyway, I was beginning to suffocate in that room. For want of something to do, I thought of writing a letter to Big Brother: at least, in this way I could make Mama happy. I picked up a piece of paper and a pencil and asked Uncle Ardeshir, "What's the date?"

Mahmud Khan's pal chipped in, "The fifth of Zi-Qa'deh."[*]

He pronounced the letters *qaf* and *ain* with such force that the brownish spots on his face grew darker. I was fit to bust laughing. Then he continued his remarks to Mahmud Khan: "I said to them, sir, that the waiving of all conceivable options has been granted by both parties." The last syllable of all his words finished in an *-ah* sound, whether appropriate or not, and he articulated exactly like some famous preacher.

At the top of the page I wrote "5th of Zi-Qa'deh," and then I wrote down the words of this fellow, followed by Mahmud Khan's remarks, "Excellent! Well done! You might also add 'Even a fraudulent option although it be gross...' Ha-ha-ha ... ha-ha." Just like a young goat. "Ha-ha, ye-e-es, ha-ha-ha."

My intention was to reproduce the remarks of these two without looking at what I was writing; but however hard I tried, I couldn't do it and instead found myself writing out the conjugation of the Arabic paradigm "to strike."

Uncle Ardeshir stood up and we were on our way. Mahmud Khan made a polite but perfunctory suggestion that we should go to his house for lunch, but I said, "I have an exam, I've got to be going."

It was obvious that he thought I was being difficult again. But at the back of his mind he calculated that if he said so, we might stay and he'd have to go to the trouble of having us for lunch—so he forgave me this time, merely saying, "Why don't you get married, girl?"

I no longer got mad at him.

When we got to the door, Mahmud Khan's chum said, "Western cigarettes? You can afford them! You bigshots can afford them! Ha-ha-ha, you certainly can!"

---

[*] He refers to the eleventh Islamic lunar month rather than the ordinary Iranian solar calendar.

I turned and saw that Mahmud Khan was offering my precious cigarettes around—my precious cigarettes, if you please! And this creature wants to give me lessons in good manners. It drives you nuts!

In a loud voice I began again to conjugate my Arabic word "to strike": "I strike, you strike, he/she/it strikes, we strike…"

I couldn't think of any other insult at that moment.

The Party

With my hair parted in the center and the two rolls which the hairdresser had arranged on either side of my head, I looked exactly like the Dutch-girl trademark they stick on cocoa packets. In addition, Mama insisted I should wear my pink dress which accentuated the shine on the tip of my nose and the redness of my cheeks. What I really wanted was a crooked parting, with my hair hanging down over my face, a pale, matte complexion, and Mama's black, sequined dress.

As a matter of fact, whenever I've wanted to look nice, I've always ended up looking worse. In short, I've never been able to carry it off. I put a flask of Nina Ricci perfume in my bag and covered a piece of cottonwool in as much powder as it would take, before wrapping it in my handkerchief. Then I was ready to set out. But who should turn up but Big Brother and his wife, and Simin and her husband!

Brother said, "Yuck! What did you get yourself up like this for!?"

(I just wish you could see Big Brother's own get-up. With that English checked jacket and a pipe in the corner of his mouth, he tries to make himself daily more and more like Uncle Ardeshir. And yet his resemblance to Uncle is in my opinion no indication that he has the right pedigree. As a matter of fact, on the contrary, I think he's making himself the image of Uncle because of his own low breeding, and a desire to worm his way into the hearts of Mama and Uncle Ardeshir.)

His wife Maliheh smiled and said, "Why're you always picking on her? You look very nice, dear."

I was afraid she might give me a "God bless you!" like her mother, but she didn't. Maliheh's resemblance to her mother is even more appalling than my brother's to Uncle Ardeshir.

I stuck my tongue out at Big Brother but I really meant it for Maliheh, because her talk gets on my nerves even more than his nonsense.

"Come here," said Simin, "and let me smoothe out your eyebrows."

I shot back, "They don't need it, leave 'em alone." But I went over to her, all the same.

She asked, "Where're you off to?"

"Mehri's place. Her brother's just got back from abroad and they're giving him a party."

My brother chipped in here, "Giving a wha-a-at!? D'ya have to start mixing Western phrases in your speech?"

As a matter of fact, "party" isn't a Western word. The Mehri family's old maid-servant actually said on the telephone this morning, "Miss Mehri is having a party this evening."

You never know where you are with my brother: at one time, he'll swallow something whole, at another he'll make a mountain out of a molehill. But when I'm involved, he'll never let anything pass. And yet when Uncle Ardeshir mixes dozens of tongue-twisting foreign words in his speech, my brother nods his head at him as a sign of approval and admiration and hastens to answer him in exactly the same terms. I really believe that the reason why my brother—and the rest of the family too—tend to think of Uncle Ardeshir as a man of education is because of these Western words which are always in his mouth. But if poor little me ventures to utter the word "party" (which even Mehri's old nanny knows), they all feel they need to look it up in Haim's Dictionary.

Simin's husband said, "In my day, there was a term of abuse, *aparty*, meaning "crook." "Party" must mean much the same thing."

You must be joking !!

Anyway, if Uncle Ardeshir is the scholar of the family, Simin's husband is the resident joker. When he opens his mouth, all his fangs protrude. Everybody sniggered at this, and I started cleaning my nails.

When Simin had had her laugh she said, "Aw, c'mon! Don't pick on the child."

"Pick on *me*? Huh!"

Mama said, "You're going to be late. Get going."

She sounded just like the starter's pistol going off at the beginning of a race but then said, "Hold it, girl! You're not leaving like this, without saying goodbye?"

I rapidly bade everyone farewell, with a kiss for Mama and Simin and Maliheh.

"Aren't you giving *me* a kiss?" asked Brother.

"No!"

Simin's husband: "What about me?"

I shot back, "Not for you either. You've got a beard."

He said, "I bet there'll be a lot of guys without beards at the party, eh?"

Get lost!

Really! What right does this lot have to laugh at nothing—but they all did laugh, except Mama. She doesn't like this type of joke from Simin's husband; or rather, when I'm in the room she doesn't like them, because she's afraid I'll get cheeky. I don't like them either, not because they get me all fired up but because they disgust me. Even his other sorts of jokes are all secondhand and half-baked.

As I got to the door, Mama asked, "Did you take a handkerchief?" Just like a school-teacher inspecting me for cleanliness. I'm surprised she didn't ask me about my drinking-cup.*

I felt like saying, "I did take one and I wrapped a powder puff in it." But Mama is an enemy of powder because she says, "Powder is an enemy of the skin." I've never managed to explain to Mama that she must be the only person in the world who likes a shiny nose and rosy cheeks.

Anyway, I didn't mention my powder puff and took off like a bullet.

∞　∞　∞

As I came in, the first person to catch my eye was Mahin. Lanky and awkward, she was dancing with Mehri's brother. Do you know what I like about Mahin? Her nerve. We were on bad terms at one time, but at the geometry exam she came and sat beside me and kept an eye on what I was writing the whole damn time. And so it went on. On the present occasion, too, her voice was raised and she was taking long strides on the dance floor, and it didn't worry her a bit that everybody was looking at her and laughing.

Not only me, everyone else who arrived noticed Mahin first. Forget the noise of her laughter: her dress was as jazzy as the patchwork quilt on old Khanom Jan's *korsi*.**

I felt sorry for Mehri's brother, poor kid! I bet Mehri had forced him to dance with Mahin, because I know he's a great one for pretty girls. He's not much to look at himself, but everybody says he's a snappy dresser. This evening, too, he was wearing a tight-fitting jacket and an incredibly wide tie. He was constantly looking all around him, trying to spot a pretty girl, and I swear he was praying fervently that no one should notice him dancing with Mahin.

I went in search of Mehri but she had disappeared and no one knew where. I have to tell you that when I come into a crowd, I get very anxious, especially where I don't know a lot of people. I think the reason

---

*The reference is to the drinking vessel taken to school by each pupil.

** In use until recent times, the *korsi* was a low table, heated from below by a brazier and covered with cloths (to retain the heat) under which people placed their legs in winter while eating, playing games, etc. on the table top.

31

for this is that I've always been close to our Mama, and have been left behind by the onward march of civilization. I've also discovered many other faults and defects due to hanging around Mama. Anyway, my anxieties started. I went looking for people I knew, and saw Homa. She was sitting in a corner and being very careful not to disturb her hairdo: when she wanted to move her head, she turned the whole upper body to right or left like someone suffering from a stiff neck. Even when she didn't move, it was really funny: she would raise her cigarette to her lips and lower it again with a movement of the hand like a clockwork doll, while the rest of the body didn't move an inch. I went and stood beside her. A heap of ash had collected by the leg of her chair. I've always hated this pink dress of mine but as I approached Homa, I positively longed to hide behind one of the chairs, so that no one should see me. The color of my dress next to the fiery red of Homa's was about as exciting as the spittle of a corpse. Homa looked as if she had walked straight out of the pages of a fashion magazine. I was absolutely devastated.

With her overly sweet smile Homa turned towards me and asked, "Wanna cigarette?"

I took a scared glance around me. Since the day when I got a slap on the wrist from Mahmud Khan over smoking, I had never dared to light up again. I noticed everyone was smoking here, so I plucked up courage and said, "Yeah!"

I realized she couldn't bend down, so I got the cigarette out of her bag myself.

My eye fell upon Sharareh, standing behind Homa. Parviz was there, too, leaning over her and looking at her amorously. All the boys I know have unfailingly fallen in love with Sharareh, at least for a few minutes. You know what I would really like? I'd really like to have Mahin's nerve, Homa's *chic*, and Sharareh's good looks. Then, of course, my name would be Sophia Loren.

I began to study Sharareh closely, as she constantly sat down and got up. She was beating time to the music with her foot, and alternately twisting her fingers together and running them through her hair. It was a lifeless sort of beauty, always (as now) without warmth. I suppose I should say that all kids are like this, but Sharareh—being beautiful— catches the eye more readily.

Parviz bent over to pick up his drink from the table and, in doing so, cut off my view of Sharareh. Darn! Just when I was mentally rehearsing one of her mannerisms. I stretched my neck in the hope of seeing her, but Rokhsar came and stood right in front of me and said,

32

"What'ya lookin' at? Why didn't ya come to Mozhi's birthday party? You can't imagine what happened…"

I paid no attention to what Rokhsar was saying, because I knew that nothing whatsoever had happened at Mozhi's birthday party. Rokhsar always talks in this inane, confused way, so that people, places, and events all become jumbled up in one's head, and you keep having to ask, "Who said this to who? Why? Where?"

Rokhsar was still talking a blue streak. However, even if I'd wanted to listen to her, I couldn't have done so: the sound of the music was too loud.

Somebody pulled Rokhsar by the sleeve from behind. Another person gave me a drink, but since the evening when I disgraced myself drinking whiskey, I had resolved never to let my lips touch liquor again.

I asked Rokhsar, "Wannit?"

"I've got one."

The boy who was behind Rokhsar, and had pulled her by the sleeve, broke in, "I wannit."

"You know each other?" intervened Rokhsar. "My brother."

Until that evening I had never seen Rokhsar's brother, but I knew Mehri had a crush on him. Mehri herself had told me and she had made a big production about his good looks.

We tried to shake hands, which was the most absurd and difficult thing we could have done. In fact, before we could actually do it, we had to make our way past any number of hands and heads and bodies.

Eventually, Rokhsar's brother piped up, "Cigarette?"

I pointed to my own cigarette which was by now nothing but a long tube of ash.

His next question was, "Dance?"

I shrugged my shoulders.

This took place while the records were being changed.

I prayed fervently that the next dance would be one I knew.

On the other side of the room, Mahin yelled, "Why doncha leave the record alone?"

Another character turned out the main light in the room. Rokhsar's brother seized me round the waist and led me into the center of the room. My dress became rucked up behind. I tried to pull it down somehow but no go! Rokhsar's brother wrestled with me to make me stand up straight while I struggled to pull my dress down, because Mehri had noticed it and was giving me long, hard stares about it. Once again, I shrugged my shoulders to make clear to her that it wasn't my fault.

My dance partner complained, "What d'ya keep shruggin' yer shoulders like that for? That all you can do?"

I had no answer. Anyway, I didn't know whether to address someone I'd only just met informally or in a formal style.[*]

I really didn't want to dance with Rokhsar's brother—first for Mehri's sake, and second because of my dress and the rolls in my hair. What I really wanted was for Firuz to come, so that we could sit in a corner and talk. He was my sort of person, that is to say he had been at one time. But I hadn't seen him for two years. In other words, I hadn't seen him since the time he went to Europe with Mehri's brother.

Back to Rokhsar's brother again: "Where ya goin' after this?"

"Home," I answered.

"We're goin' to the *Kolbeh*.[**] Ya comin'?"

"No. Have to get home."

He turned to a boy I didn't know and said, "This chick's weird. She wants to go home after this."

The other boy said, "No! That right?"

And both looked at me pityingly. I was very peeved at this. I really wanted to say something very stinging but nothing came to mind. All I did was kick Rokhsar's brother in the leg.

Sharareh and Mehri's brother had their faces glued together and were hardly moving. It was as though they were waiting for someone to come and take their picture. I was sure Parviz had made a declaration of his love and Sharareh was now working on Mehri's brother. I couldn't help laughing.

Rokhsar's brother asked, "What ya laughin' at?"

I almost shrugged my shoulders again but stopped myself in time.

A gentleman of a certain age, totally unknown to me, was standing at one corner of the dance floor, with his eyes riveted on mine. There was no room for me to get out of his line of vision. He had a dirty little Melvyn Douglas-mustache. I think he'd also oiled his hair. Ugh! What a sorry lot these old-time gigolos are! For a couple of moments he

---

[*] Like, for example, French German, and Spanish, Persian has formal and informal constructions for "you" when addressing others.

[**] Literally "cottage" or "hut." It was the name of a very high-class nightclub in Tehran during the 1960s and 70s.

slipped away and left me in peace: he'd gone to stop the record and put on some Valentino tango. But by the time he'd got back to the edge of the dance floor, the kids had changed the record again. Only this fellow was more pathetic than me at Mehri's party.

And still Firuz hadn't come.

The dance came to an end. I went over to Mehri who was standing beside Hosain and a girl I didn't know. Hosain, as usual, was shooting his mouth off about his latest conquests of girls. Nobody was there to ask Hosain—with all these girls running after him—why his eyes and heart were always chasing after other girls.

I took Mehri aside.

Hosain called out, "Hi, dearie."

"Dearie," you can stuff it!! My flesh creeps at this expression. I knew that as soon as we'd turned our backs, he'd boast to the girl beside him how he once picked up both Mehri and myself.

Mehri said, "Where've you been? I couldn't see you."

"You saw me perfectly well. I was dancing with Rokhsar's brother."

"Did you like him?"

"No."

Mehri was very cheered at this and said, "Yeah, he's not your type. He's very dim."

"*You* like him!"

"Oh well, I like the dim ones."

During the day Mehri is one person till 4 p.m. and a different one afterwards. Until four o'clock she either consults the poems of Hafez for guidance[*] or holds forth on the artistic genius of Charlie Chaplin. If she reads a detective story, she wraps it in a newspaper and labels it *Lamartine's Poems.*[**] One day, at school, she sobbed from early morning till four o'clock on learning that Beethoven had gone deaf. From four o'clock onwards she would hum "yeah-yeah-yeah" and start jiving and performing all the latest steps.

I asked, "Didn't you invite Firuz?"

She let her eye rove around the room and said, "He didn't come. He's easy enough to spot. You never told me how things stand—

---

[*] Hafez (14th century), often regarded as Iran's premier lyric poet, is commonly used for the mundane purpose of taking auguries.

[**] The French poet Alphonse de Lamartine (1790-1869) was greatly admired in Iran as one of the pre-eminent poets of the European Romantic movement.

remember? You know everything about me, but you never tell me anything."

Mehri just has to worm everybody's secrets out—even those things which can't be told. Of course, you understand there are all sorts of things which a person can't talk about. For example, the business with Firuz merely amounted to this: the last evening before he went away he was a guest in our house, together with all the relatives. Mama sent me to get some ice. I had just picked up the ice-container when Firuz came into the kitchen. He came straight up to me and gave me a big kiss. I was really taken unawares, for I was not expecting anything like it. Until that evening Firuz and I had only dealt with each other through the written word, that is to say I had borrowed and read most of his books. I have to admit that I often placed Firuz and myself in the situation of the central characters in these books, but I had never imagined that Firuz liked me. When he kissed me, I really enjoyed it. I enjoyed it so much that I stuck my face out and kissed him back—a noisy, spit-laden kiss. Firuz wiped his face and laughed. You'd have thought I'd done something funny, whereas it was the most serious thing I'd ever done up to that moment.

In short, this incident remained in my heart and even grew. I longed to see him, to see what Firuz thought of me. If only I could show him, somehow or other, that—if I wanted to—I knew how to kiss like Shirley MacLaine.

O.K., but how could I tell such things to Mehri? She'd never understand. And even if she did, she'd never believe that someone like me could kiss in the Shirley MacLaine manner.

At this point, someone asked, "Like to dance?"

"No," I replied.

He said, "What a bore." I had no idea who it was, for my eyes were glued to the door.

Pari and Mamal were droning away together in English, close to my ear—Pari with an American accent and Mamal with a Persian one. My brother ought to have been there! And it wasn't only Pari and Mamal: foreign languages were as thick as cigarette-smoke.

Mehri said, "Come along, my uncle wants to meet you."

Mehri's uncle was the fellow with the Douglas mustache and the oiled hair. I had nothing to say.

I ended up asking him if he could dance Lazgi-style,[*] and then I gave him a hard look.

A woman with the figure of a doorpost came to my rescue. She shoved a plate of food into "uncle's" hand and said, "Get on and eat your dinner."

Mehri explained, "My uncle's wife."

I got a kick out of saying, "Really?" and grinned at the doorpost. However, she looked at me as if to say, "Keep your hands off my husband—or else…!" For his part, "uncle" turned his naughty old eyes away from me, with a glance as if to say, "See what we married men have to put up with!"

In the middle of the room waves of color and smoke were oscillating, and I could no longer see the door for heads and elbows blocking the view.

And then someone shouted, "Hey, Firuz has turned up."

I felt as though I was once again holding the bowl of ice and standing in the middle of the kitchen. All the remarks I had been rehearsing for this meeting completely went out of my head. I took a couple of steps in the direction indicated by Mehri and ran smack into Firuz's chest. The smell of his perfume got up my nose. The buckle on his belt was the size of a plate, and the curl he had stuck down in the middle of his forehead must have taken hours to arrange. Furthermore, he had his teeth clamped round a cigar as big as himself. My head was spinning worse than on the day when I had drunk whiskey while Big Brother was present.

So that was the end of Firuz! Too bad! What a nice boy he used to be. Dead and buried, good and proper. Anyway, for the first time in history, the corpse himself was present at the shrouding and interment ceremonies, large as life, smartly dressed and wearing perfume.

I never have any luck. If someone comes up to me at a party, it's bound to be Mehri's uncle. If I practice the Shirley MacLaine kiss for two years in front of the mirror, for a certain person, who bobs up but this new Firuz!

On my way home I remembered that the powder puff was still in my handkerchief. I threw it out of the window of the car, and shook the handkerchief out on the car floor.

---

[*] The Lazgis (also Lesghians) are a fiercely independent mountain tribe living in Daghestan, to the west of the Caspian Sea. They have always been a minor thorn in the side of the central administration. The question here is akin to asking someone in North America whether he or she can do a hillbilly dance.

The Women's Mourning Ceremony

It had been arranged that the women's mourning rites should be held at our house. This was on the very Friday when Mehri and I had fixed to sit down and prepare our chemistry assignment—or rather, we had fixed for Mehri to have lunch at my place, then study until six, and afterwards go to the movies. Ugh! All because of that Grandma of mine. When she was alive she was a nuisance, and she still was now that she was dead. Of course, now she was dead, I ought not to talk like this. A few days ago, I can't remember what I said, but everybody flared up, shouting, "Don't speak ill of the dead!" But as for me, I never liked her while she was alive, and I told her to her face. Now she's dead, I still don't like her and I'll say so behind her back. But if they hear me talking this way, they'll give me such a slap in the chops that I won't know whether I'm going or coming. When she was alive, nobody else liked her either, right? They all used to say she had a bad mouth, she was stingy and a nasty person. But from the day she died, no one could recall anything but good of her. They speak of her as though she were the Immaculate Lady of Qom herself.[*] They all claim to have heard the words she uttered with her last breath, and they hold them like votive dates in the palm of their hand and offer them to each other.[**] Everyone's recollection of her last wise words differed, and none of them resembled the sort of things Grandma would say. If you ask me what she said before she died, I'll tell you, she certainly said, "Hey, you quarrelsome creature Roqiyeh, what's this you bought—meat or dog's mess? God curse you!" or something like that. Anyone who knew Grandma will know that what she said was this sort of thing, not "Oh God, I entrust my dear little ones into Your hands!" or "Oh Imam Ali, be the friend and support of my children!"

Grandma was always cursing her "dear little ones" for having their eyes on what she would leave them.

---

[*] The Persian term is Ma'sumeh ("pure/chaste"), an epithet commonly reserved for Fatemeh, daughter of the Seventh Imam and Sister of the Eighth, whose shrine is visited in Qom.

[**] As an act of piety, it is common practice to dedicate food (specifically dates) for the use of the poor at certain religious seasons, and such offerings naturally acquire a special aura of their own.

And perhaps she was right! Have I told you what Auntie Fakhri and Uncle Hasan said—what they were saying that day in the hospital, in the final days when Grandma was going downhill?

I didn't tell you? I was sitting with Auntie Fakhri and Uncle Hasan on a bench in the hospital garden, waiting for Mama and Uncle Ardeshir to come out of Grandma's room, so that we might all go home together. Grandma's ring was on my aunt's hand. I said to her, "How well it looks on your hand, Auntie!"

I expected my aunt to be pleased, but Uncle Hasan didn't give her a chance to speak but said, "Shame on you! At least you might have waited another few days before getting your claws into things."

Auntie piped up in her thin voice, "What for? Should I wait for these few trinkets to go to the whorish wife of His Lordship Hosain? Or should I leave them for the shrewish bitch you'll take one day? Anyway, there's no question, her bits and pieces belong to me."

"What good are they to you, woman?" asked Uncle Hasan. "At your age you can't wear jewelry anymore. Maybe you're gonna hide them in the lining of your panties?"

I burst out laughing at Uncle's joke, but from Auntie's look I realized that these two were not joking.

Auntie said, "Dirt be…" and indicated "on your head!" with her hand.

Uncle Hasan replied, "No! Seriously, what good are they to you? Do you think you're really young? Do you think you're really beautiful, for crying out loud?"

I've already told you, I think, that Auntie Fakhri imagines she *is* still young and beautiful. Whenever something bad happens to her, she quotes, "'The peacock must suffer for its plumage.' Whatever I have to go through, my dear, I put up with for the sake of my youth and beauty." The whole family has heard that one. Mama herself is always saying, "Forget what that little girl Fakhri looks like now—she never was beautiful." And Simin's husband adds maliciously, "She was never young either!" Anyway, be that as it may, Auntie herself imagines she is young and beautiful, and that's why she was hurt by Uncle's remarks. She raised her voice another octave and said, "Even if you had eight eyes—eight!—you'd still be jealous, you good-for-nothing! Those who want to see my youth and beauty can see them well enough."

Uncle Hasan sniggered.

I, too, was about to laugh and put a stop to all this but I couldn't. I began to feel queasy. I always feel queasy at the smell of hospitals. I don't know why, but I was on the point of throwing up when Mama and Uncle Ardeshir appeared and we left.

Well, then, I was telling you how I became furious when the women's mourning rites were fixed to be held in our house. And do you know the real reason why they had to take place there? Because Auntie's reception room is too small and the building where she lives doesn't have a travertine facade. Then, again, Uncle Hosain has some piddling official appointment and is out of the country with all his brood. As for my Uncle Hasan, he is a sort of professional wandering dervish, with no proper home or life style, who permanently lives in hotels. I tell you, whenever I plan something, some disaster or other has to drop from on high and upset my program.

I'd had it in mind to sit down that morning and study. However, Maliheh arrived early to lend Mama a hand, and I got roped in as her girl Friday. Later Auntie Fakhri turned up, only to walk round and round me, buttering me up to keep bringing her more cucumber salad. They didn't give me time to breathe, let alone study. Lucky Simin, pregnant and in her final days: *she's* lying in bed at home!

Khanom Jan arrived for lunch, which we ate in Big Brother's former room because the table and chairs had all been moved out of the dining room for the ceremony. Ugh! How dreary an empty room looks: just from its gloomy appearance it was obvious that a death had occurred. In other respects, however, everybody was as busy about their affairs and as excited as on the evening of the betrothal of Big Brother and Maliheh.

In short, the whole day was spent entertaining, and I wasn't able to open my book before the afternoon. It all had me worried about the exam on Saturday.

When we'd finished lunch, Simin's husband appeared on the scene, accompanied by Uncle Ardeshir. He mumbled something in Mama's ear and she cried out, "Oh my God, I could die. Surely it wasn't due yet? Has she gone to the hospital?"

Simin's husband nodded, "Of course. Get up and let's go."

Mama rejoined, "Can't be done. What will I do about the mourning ceremony?" Nevertheless, she did get up.

Simin's husband shrugged his shoulders. The whole business had left him really floored. I prayed fervently that the mourning ceremony wouldn't come off.

"After all, my dear," Uncle intervened, "you can't leave the child alone at such a time. Her mother must be at her side."

I piped up with relish, "You mean Simin is giving birth?"

Mama and Uncle and Simin's husband all cried "Shush!" together. It was as if the word "birth" in my mouth was a dirty expression. The air was pregnant with "shushes."

Khanom Jan interposed, "We can manage here. Maliheh is here, Fakhr-e Zaman[*] is here—and when all is said and done, it's Fakhr-e Zaman's mother who has died, my dear, so she's the chief mourner."

As long as she was eating cucumber salad, Auntie Fakhri was oblivious to the fact that she was an important person in the mourning ritual. Now she suddenly became aware of her own importance and cried out, in a most ridiculous, artificial tone, "Oh, my poor mother!"

I burst out laughing, and this time they all gave me dirty looks again.

Auntie Fakhri gave a sniff. "The lady-of-the-house is the chief mourner and must sit above the rest." However, it was obvious that she wouldn't mind having an exalted position all to herself.

At this, Uncle Ardeshir turned to me and said, "Very well, you too ought to sit up there next to Fakhr-e Zaman, and be a chief mourner."

There is no problem for which Uncle Ardeshir does not have the solution up his sleeve. For all his trite remarks, he's a kindly man and never hesitates for a moment to deal with difficult situations. Everybody now agreed, "He's right!"

Ha! Sure enough, he was right! Uncle only has to issue a ruling for the rest of them to ratify it. I still longed for somebody, just once, to cut across Uncle's pronouncements, and of course not to talk the same sort of nonsense as Uncle himself does.

"Let's go, Madam," pleaded Simin's husband, "we'll be too late."

Mama refused to be pushed, but first went to her room. I followed her and asked, "Mama, what exactly do I have to do?"

Mama took her dark-blue and white dress out of the closet. "Sit right there and don't move until the ceremony is over," she said. "Hand me a pair of stockings."

"Are you goin' to get your black dress out too?"

"Don't ask so many stupid questions, child! I'm not going to visit my little girl in a black dress. She's givin' birth, it would be enough to give her a fit. And watch your tongue in the other room. Do my zipper up."

---

[*] This is the more formal version of the name we have hitherto encountered as Fakhri. It means "Pride of the Age."

I pulled up her zipper, but still continued to ask, "So, what am I supposed to do?"

Simin's husband heard me from the other room and imitated me in a whining tone, "What am I supposed to do? Ugh! Good grief! You aren't a little baby, are you? When your sister was your age she was married."

In fact, and in the first place, she was older at that time. Secondly, they've got this new idea from somewhere of calling me a "little baby," while at the same time implying that a bitter old maid will soon be left at home on the shelf. I guess it comes from Simin's husband, and this mean trick on the part of a man who listens to everybody's tattle really leaves one at a loss for words. Anyway, they left and I returned to Big Brother's former room to ask our Khanom Jan what I was supposed to do. By now, they were talking about a *men's* mourning ceremony. I couldn't interrupt. Uncle held forth, "In all fairness, it was very dignified. Poor Erfaq od-Dowleh sat there from beginning to end, but he really had grown old. Of course, I hadn't seen him for some years. Mobayyeni too."

At this Khanom Jan chipped in, "Our own Mr. Mobayyeni? Well, he's getting on, he sure is getting on in years, my friend."

Uncle Ardeshir replied, "He's older than Aunt Shazdeh, isn't he? He must be about your age, Khanom Jan."

Khanom Jan turned to Auntie Fakhri: "I've gone stone-deaf. Can't hear a thing."

Dear old Khanom Jan: her deafness is always a convenience. Whenever people say something she has no intention of answering, she immediately becomes stone-deaf. For several years now this has been her practice, and she always speaks of her deafness with amazement as if to say, "Just a few moments ago I was hearing fine." Sometimes, on the other hand, she claims to be deaf in order to be able to give the answers she particularly has in mind. At such times, if she happens to catch my eye, she winks at me. Khanom Jan is a real sweetheart.

Uncle Ardeshir was still talking a blue streak—about a bunch of people who, it seemed, ought all to be mourned themselves any day soon now.

Auntie Fakhri asked, "Well then, who was the one to wind up the mourning ceremony?"

"The Very Reverend Behbehani."

In a self-satisfied tone she said, "So, you finally found him then."

I was still shifting from one foot to the other, hoping they'd stop talking for a moment so that I could clear up my own responsibility. But do you think I could?

Uncle replied to Auntie's question, "Well, ye-e-es … But I don't think it was absolutely necessary to bring in the Reverend Behbehani. In fact, things nearly went badly wrong. It was all the fault of that bigmouth Hasan, who insisted on bringing this fellow in. He telephoned him again and again until he got hold of him—but only at the last minute. There wasn't even an opportunity to tell him who the dead person was. He arrived out of breath, and went straight up into the pulpit and began to enumerate the moral virtues of the deceased. However, when he said, "I myself had close and affectionate ties to the dear late one," I noticed Hasan turn pale. Anyway, we explained to the clergyman that he'd got it wrong, and that the dead person—now with God—had been a virtuous woman and *never* had close relations with *anyone* after the death of her husband, let alone with the Reverend Behbehani himself!"

Uncle Ardeshir does belly-laughs, and on this occasion his belly really went up and down. I laughed too, but Auntie Fakhri gave me another dirty look.

He now continued, "If an ordinary cleric had wound up the ceremony, what difference would it have made? After all, we nearly had a scandal on our hands."

I butted in, "You said it was very dignified."

Uncle got annoyed. "Of course it was dignified! Did I just say it wasn't?"

I was rather pleased that I had upset him, so I asked Khanom Jan again, "What am I supposed to do?" I must tell you, if Uncle laughs with his belly, Khanom Jan laughs with the wrinkles under her eyes. She laughed now and said, "Your exam will turn out O.K., my dear." When she laughs like this, my heart goes out to her.

I indulged her and said gently, "No, Khanom Jan, dear. I'm not talking about the exam, but today's ceremony." (I like indulging her.) She replied, "It's nothing, dearie: just put your *chador* * on and take your place in the seat of honor."

---

* The *chador* is the general name for a modesty veil, whether it covers all or part of a woman's body. The basic meaning of the term is "tent." While commonly black or dark since the Islamic Revolution, other colors and even floral patterns have been used at various times.

43

I took great pleasure in announcing, "I haven't got a *chador*." For a moment I thought I was going to become the outcast of the family. The shocked cries of Khanom Jan and Auntie cheered me up, but Missy Maliheh—Big-Cheese Interferer-General—instructed me: "Put on your mother's *chador*!"

In short: I was caught, with no way out.

I put on Mama's *chador*, and you should've seen what a sight I looked! I felt a real fool. Mama's *chador* was too long for me and totally enveloped me. Moreover, it tended to pull my head back. I tried to hold the edges of its two borders in my teeth, but I soon gave up. My hair was absolutely standing on end, because I simply can't bear to have a bit of cloth or rubber or paper between my teeth, and when I do, that makes my hair stand on end. I don't know how others manage to do this. Take the case of Mehri's old maid-servant, she's always got the corner of her *chador* between her teeth. Yuck!

Anyway, I went and sat at the far end of the room, that is to say I was *made* to sit there, exactly like a stewed eggplant. You think my problems were over at this point? Not on your life! This was only the beginning. It was like this: poor little me had never learned to sit cross-legged. My two knees kept shooting up like a scarecrow's arms in a harvest field. However hard I tried to keep them on the floor, it was no go! My knees kept popping up and down one after the other, and with all my struggling under the *chador*, I must've looked like a black crow flapping its wings. In any case, I cut a very poor figure indeed.

Auntie came and sat next to me saying, "Stop wriggling and pull your *chador* over your face."

How on earth could I stop wriggling? I pulled my *chador* right over my face and then couldn't see a thing. However, somehow or other, I made a narrow gap between the two edges in front of one of my eyes and stared at the door.

They came in dribs and drabs—mighty strange women I'd never seen before, though I did recognize the odd one here and there. Each one as she arrived sat down by the door right away. All around me and Auntie and dear old Khanom Jan was empty space, but by the door there was an absolute mob.

Maliheh was killing herself trying to get the crowd to move up, but however much she urged them, they would protest, "No, no, please excuse, that's much too high up for me." Eventually, all the space was taken up, or rather that the half-circle of room which I could see became filled up. When it was finally full, Auntie let out a loud scream. I thought she must've been stung by a wasp. In alarm, I threw my *chador* back and asked, "What's the matter, Auntie?"

Auntie was furious with me because she was all set to start weeping and I, with my ill-timed question, had really spoilt everything. It took a moment for Auntie to compose herself once more, and then she let out two or three screams in succession and began to sob, "Boohoo! Boohoo!…"

I felt certain everybody would realize now that Auntie was putting on an act of crying. I shook her by the arm and whispered, "Don't, Auntie Fakhri! They'll all know what you're doing, and it looks bad."

Auntie gave me one of those looks which Maliheh's mother sometimes gives people. They make you wish you were a bug clinging to the wall. She also shook my hand off her own and went on with her boohooing. This time she was more skillful at it and was really into her stride. After every couple of boohoos she would add something like, "Oh poor me, I've lost my mother" or, "Oh wretched me, I haven't a soul in the world!"

I was so embarrassed at Auntie's antics that I didn't want to look anyone in the eye, but covertly I noticed that the whole gathering were swaying right and left, and forwards and backwards, in time with Auntie Fakhri's boohoos. I nearly burst out laughing. The worst part was that I caught the eye of Mehri, who was sitting in the crowd with her mother.

Auntie was banging her knees vigorously, and I jumped in the air like a firecracker at the smacking noise. For a moment my laughter was under control, but then it got worse. Whatever I did, I was unable to stop. At that time, when a laughing fit came over me, I used to stare at my thumb, and the laughter would die down. Lately whenever I do this I start remembering Mozhi's thumb. Have you ever seen Mozhi's thumb? It's had a real good knock, just like Mansur Khan's noggin. Anyway, on this occasion, my trick only made matters worse, not better.

I tried not to look at Mehri but it didn't work. Just in time I remembered my *chador*, which had slipped down to my shoulders as Aunt Fakhri let out her first scream. I pulled it back over my head and went on laughing quietly under it.

I thought, "Heaven forbid everybody else should think I was crying." The very thought put a stop to my laughter, because in that case I'd be just like Auntie, and that's one thing I did *not* want to be. After all, nobody would!

I was sweating under the *chador* and my legs had gone to sleep. I looked out of the folds at Mehri and saw that she was looking at me. I began by asking her with a silent movement of my lips, "Have you done any studying?" She asked back, with a movement of her head, "Whatya say?" I now tried to say in a strangled voice, "Chemistry. Did you prepare your chemistry?"

I couldn't understand what she was saying because Maliheh was busy placing a water-pipe in front of Mrs. Erfaq od-Dowleh and blocking my view of Mehri. I took a stealthy sideways look to catch sight of her, but Auntie gave me a dig in the ribs. I tried to think of something to make her really annoyed, but then told myself to forget it.

One of Mama's distant cousins, who was sitting beside me, started to slurp her coffee. At first, I thought she must've fallen asleep and was snoring. I don't know why every little thing was making me laugh, but it nearly happened again. Then I noticed that some characters opposite me were weeping. I tell you, they were really weeping! They were doing it with such ease that one couldn't help envying them. They really seemed to be enjoying their work.

One lady who was the image of a worm-eaten quince and had a mustache as well, was talking to Aunt Shazdeh.

Aunt Shazdeh was leaning towards the Worm-eaten Quince and listening so attentively that I fancied that side of her head must be nothing but a big, fat ear. I couldn't hear a word they were saying.

There were two others, talking away to my right, and them I couldn't see. One of them said, "No! You don't say, my dear! What did the girl do then?" The second speaker replied, "A real slippery character, you can't even imagine: she's got the boy in such a tight corner that he is about to marry her. But there you are, just as I said, another week and we'll be having a wedding. But the bride, my dear,…"

At this point Auntie let out another shriek, and so I didn't get the rest of it. Still another person was saying something about her milliner, but I couldn't understand what she was driving at.

Apart from the little group who were having a good time weeping, the rest were chattering together tête-à-tête. However, whatever they were doing, they never forgot to rock their bodies hither and thither. The room looked just like a scene from a film about the life of penguins, which I'd seen some time before, together with Rokhsar and her brother.

The molla was busy in the hallway, chanting away at passages from the Koran and prayers of lamentation. It was most affecting, and I really felt sorry for him because nobody was paying the least attention to his plaintive call.

The room was hot as hell. The crowd did not diminish, but grew from moment to moment. The ceremony went on so long that I thought it'd never end. But eventually it did; that is to say the molla brought it to a close. Abruptly he cut short his lamentations, recited a few Persian maxims, and then the session turned informal. In twos and threes they stood up and left, and the room was suddenly deserted. Just a few relatives and family-members whom I knew stayed on.

I asked Khanom Jan, "Can I go now?"

"Run along, dearie," she replied, "go and splash a drop of water on your face."

I wanted to say that I hadn't wept a single tear, but Khanom Jan winked at me.

My legs had gone to sleep and I was limping. As I reached the door, Erfaq od-Dowleh's daughter was saying to Auntie Fakhri, "That was a very fine ceremony! Very warm indeed. You made a really dignified thing of it."

Aunt Shazdeh added, "How well you spoke, dear. God bless you!"

Auntie Fakhri took on a self-satisfied look, as if to say, "No big deal."

∞   ∞   ∞

I went downstairs. Uncle Ardeshir asked, "How did it go?"

I was about to answer him in his own former words, "It was very dignified," but instead I just said, "It went off fine."

Naming Simin's Baby

If you only knew what comical contortions they got into over naming Simin's new child. Everybody was playing his or her own tune. Now that Uncle Ardeshir has established his claim to be an expert on things Western, he occasionally gets the whim to demonstrate that he knows Persian better than anybody else. So he went and practically killed himself trying to find a name for Simin's child in the *Shahnamah.** And what names: Haftvad, Kharad, Gostaham, Arjasp, and Shaghad! I'd never heard of any such names as these. The only name I had heard of a similar sort was Hovakhshatarah. This is why I said, "Come on, Uncle Ardeshir, this simply won't do."

"What won't do?" he asked.

"Just think! How can one say, 'Come and do pottie, Hovakhshatarah!'? It just won't work."

Uncle's reaction was, "How's that?! What's this Hovakhshatarah business? Are you talking rubbish again?"

"Well, the names you suggested sound just like Hovakhshatarah too," I retorted.

Uncle Ardeshir, not to be put down, came back at me: "Don't talk nonsense, child. Those are all good Persian names, straight from the *Shahnamah.*"

I acknowledged that: "I know, but…"

At this Uncle asked with great contempt, "You know, do you?"

I forgot that I am not allowed to *know* anything in Uncle's presence. And I have to admit, at first I was merely guessing that he'd found the names in the *Shahnamah*. But when I saw him, in the last few days, flipping through an abbreviated version of the *Shahnamah* and mumbling words to himself, I sensed that something was going on.

I pretended that I wanted to be instructed and asked, "Those names you mentioned—what were they?"

---

* *Shahnamah* = "The Book of Kings" or "The Imperial Register," by the poet Ferdowsi: the Persian national epic, dating from about 1000 A.D. It is a vast storehouse of mythology, history, and heroic deeds, and praises the Iran of pre-Islamic days. The names chosen by the uncle are of quite obscure figures, and in some cases (Haftvad, Arjasp) by no means positive or patriotic. The name the narrator admits to knowing, Hovakhshatarah, is that of the outstanding Median ruler Cyaxares (Greek version: normal Persian, Kai-Ka'us), who reigned 625-585 B.C. Uncle Ardeshir is perhaps confounded by its somewhat strange sound to modern Iranian ears.

Uncle Ardeshir cleared his throat and recited the names distinctly, one by one, as though he were addressing some kind of donkey.

I then objected, "Who'd dare to slap the hand of a child named Shaghad or Gostaham—or that other one, what was it again? With such names it is obvious they all know karate."

Mama gave me one of those looks which mean, "Watch that long tongue of yours!" My dear old Khanom Jan had no idea what karate was, but she wrinkled up her eyes and smiled at me. Whatever I do, she always reacts in that way. I felt strongly moved to explain karate to her, but Uncle butted in, "You done your homework? Standing here, interfering in high philosophical matters!"

Whenever Uncle can't think of a blistering reply, he asks a question back and upsets you that way. I shot back, "Yes, I've done it," so that he should understand, even if I hadn't done it, it was none of his business.

There is one good thing about Uncle Ardeshir: when he flares up, one gets a real kick out of it. Anyway, even if he had been in a position to chastise me, he never got the chance, because Uncle Hosain was getting all steamed up about the name business, and Uncle Ardeshir was forced to get back into the discussion again. Now, my Uncle Hosain is the exact opposite of Uncle Ardeshir, that is to say he's never grasped that if one wants to play the European to perfection, one must first learn to play the Iranian. That was why all the names *he* proposed were out-and-out Western. It was particularly funny because he insisted on giving all the names in both their French and English forms: thus, "Georges" together with "George," "John" alongside "Jean." (I couldn't help silently adding my own contribution, "Lousy" and "Shaddup!") After all, you tell me, who's going to give their kids names like these? But no one ever feels they have to answer Uncle Hosain, because his remarks are always so wishy-washy that they are a refutation in themselves. Of course, this doesn't include Uncle Ardeshir, who feels he has to reply to everybody.

He now said, "No, sir! Neither Georges nor George: what d'you mean by such nonsense?"

Uncle Hosain retorted angrily, "All right, call him Mamdali Ja'far, so that when he goes to Europe he'll be laughed at, and no one will be able to pronounce it."

This really upset Uncle Ardeshir: "Shit on them, if they laugh at him! Blast their eyes! Let them learn to pronounce it. What're you talking about, my friend? Did they laugh at me when I was there? I forced them to pronounce my name properly."

I blurted out, "Didn't you say they used to call you 'Jim' over there?"

At this Uncle Hosain was delighted, while Ardeshir became incensed. However, Khanom Jan now changed the subject, or rather brought it back to the original point, by saying, "Give him his grandfather's name, my dear." Auntie Fakhri, of course, had wanted to give the child her father's name from the very beginning. In short, the whole business turned into a donnybrook. About one lousy name they started such a free-for-all you'd have had to see it to believe it. Finally, when they'd had a fine old shouting-match, it was decided to open the Koran at random. I don't know whose suggestion it was, but it fell to Uncle Ardeshir to consult the Holy Book. Solemnly he inspected the page from top to bottom and bottom to top and then said, "It's opened at the *Sura of Yusof.*"*

The name of one of the most recent twelve forefathers—or it may have been sixteen—was in fact Yusof. So the child was named Yusof and everybody rested easy.

If Uncle Ardeshir hadn't himself been the one to consult the Koran, I'm certain he would have insisted on the name being Hovakhshatarah. But having himself consulted the Book, he behaved as though he were the Prophet and the *Sura of Yusof* had been revealed to him personally!

Simin's husband was standing near Uncle, and said with relish, "Simin, we're lucky. If it had opened at Chapter II instead of Chapter XII, our son's name would have to be "Cow."** Then we'd have been in a fine mess!"

"Go on with you, don't make me laugh," replied Simin. "You know I can't laugh yet."

I began to wonder where Mama had dug up our names—Simin, Dadash, and Suri. Not "Dadash," of course, since that's just what we call him, "Big Brother," while his real name is Sasan. My own name is the least appropriate of the lot: Suri, that is "Rose": what sort of name is that for someone who looks like me?! Anyone who hears it and doesn't know me is bound to imagine that I am a plump young thing,

---

* While not orthodox practice, random consultation of the Koran (and other esteemed books) for guidance is very popular. The "Sura of Yusof" (= Joseph) is the 12th chapter of the Koran in the commonly accepted ordering, though Muslims usually prefer to name the chapters rather than numbering them.

** As indicated in the preceding note, each chapter is commonly referred to by a term derived from the text. In the case of Chapter II, this is "The Cow."

with a red and white complexion, blue eyes, and hair hanging down like a mass of gold braid. There was a girl in Grade Four when I was in Grade One; I don't remember what her name was, but *she* could certainly have been a Suri. Anyway, this family of mine knocked themselves out to find a name like Suri for me, while I'm the exact image of a grasshopper. The only reason they did it, I believe, was so that they could call me "Black Suri," although I'm quite happy when Khanom Jan calls me "Blackie dear," and leaves the Suri off altogether. Still, this is just quibbling. After all, my name is O.K. Just take Mozhi's name, poor kid! Her full name is Mozhegan, which means "Eyelashes," though—God help her!—she doesn't have a single eyelash to her name. Or at least the few she does have are stuck like thorns into all the styes she's afflicted with. In short, if I were in her place, I'd really be embarrassed at my name. The only good thing is that she herself is unaware of it. But to get back to the point, I've no idea where my parents got these colorless names. Still, if everybody has to go through such trouble as Simin did in naming her child, they will certainly choose something—anything—and get themselves off the hook. That's doubtless how Mama did it. I once asked her, "Where did you get our names from?"

"I didn't get them from anywhere," was her reply.

I came back, "Then how did it come about that we got the names Simin, Sasan, and Suri?"

Her answer to this was, "If I had called your brother Ramin, you'd have been Nasrin"—which in no way answered my question.

I went on to ask, "If you'd had two more children, what would you have called them?"

She didn't need to think even for a moment. "If they'd been girls and you still had the same names, they'd have been Susan and Sara; if boys, Sohrab and Siyamak. Furthermore, if you three had been Simin, Ramin, and Nasrin, they'd have been Parvin, Afshin, and stuff like that."

At this I wondered, "Why, for heaven's sake?"

"Very well, either you'd all begin with S, or you'd all end in the rhyme -*in*."*

I burst out, "That's it? How unimaginative!"

---

* The letters involved in the mother's final explanation are considered lucky in Persian folklore. However, the names themselves are usually flowers for the girls, and heroes for the boys.

I believe that Mama never thinks she can be wrong, and that was why she was upset by my remark. She retorted, "Thank God you were the last. If I'd been fated to have another two like you, I would by now have been in my grave seven times over."

At the thought of annoying Mama, I always feel a little sad. However, I know that I don't annoy her all that much, and her grumblings are never very serious. Still, I find it hard to put up with them, and at the same time, as I've told you before, I feel sad at provoking them. So I said nothing further. The only conclusion I arrived at was that if I have a child one day, I'm not going to call it Hovakhshatarah, nor give it the name of a chapter from the Koran, nor one that begins with S or ends in N, nor one with any *other* letter at the end or the beginning! You understand what I mean? What I'm trying to say is that nobody should name a child on the basis of such things. But to tell the truth, I myself don't know what name I would give. It's no good asking this bunch. In the first place, none of them knows a damn thing. Secondly, nowadays whenever I ask something, they exchange meaningful glances and suggest that my problem is I'm longing for a husband. It's enough to turn your stomach! A few days ago I said, "I've had enough of going to the seaside. This summer let's go somewhere else." Like somebody highly intelligent who—when a person merely says F.—immediately understands the reference is to Forugh Farrokhzad,* they all looked at each other and then said, "O.K., you're at an age when the least thing tries your patience. As soon as you're married, everything will be all right. We'll have to give some serious thought to your case." For God's sake, can you see any connection? If I'm fed up with the sea, what does it have to do with getting married? If I dare to ask about naming children, all hell will break loose. Nor is it any use my saying I've absolutely no intention of getting married. I've said it a few times already and seen the result. All the women in the family say, "Ha! We used to talk like that." Even Maliheh declares, "I too used to say I would never marry." Just think, for God's sake! Even Maliheh, who I know talks nonsense anyway. And, of course, I shall never understand how anyone could want to marry Big Brother. Anyone who says that he is good-looking is talking rubbish. Still, Maliheh did want him—that much I do know.

---

* A well-known Iranian woman-poet of the period between World War II and the Islamic Revolution. She was a consciously liberated woman and something of a "high liver." Farrokhzad died in a car-crash in 1967, at the age of thirty-two.

Anyway, that's beside the point. What I was saying was this: in the last few days I have gone so deeply into the matter of names and created such a stir that even Rokhsar's brother became aware of it recently. By the way, did I tell you that Rokhsar's brother has lately begun to chase after me in a big way? Our Mama, of course, tends to purse her lips at such things. People say he's too good-looking but—heavens above!— is there anything wrong with that? When talk turns to Big Brother, they always say that on one side he has good looks, on the other he has virtues. But as for that kid Rokhsar's brother, wow! He really is a looker. I'm not that crazy about him, it's just that Mama is inclined to take the fun out of things.

The point is, as I was saying, Rokhsar's brother had also noticed that I was all the time worrying my head about people's names. Everybody calls him Kiki. You know how it is. I myself have never used his name because—I don't know why—I find it hard to address people I've just got to know, by their first name, or to use the familiar form. Whenever I speak to him, I always try to use the polite form, and so on … When speaking to Mehri about him, I refer to him as "Rokhsar's brother." A few days ago I actually asked him, "They call you Kiki, but what's your real name?"

He answered with his own question, "What's the matter with you these days? Everyone you meet you start asking them what their name means or who gave it to them."

It wasn't that I didn't want to answer him, but I couldn't think of a way to put it so that he would understand. So in the end I said nothing. Finally he revealed, "My real name is Kayumars," but it was obvious that he was annoyed with me. After that we never spoke on the phone again. I don't really care, yet (I don't know why) I feel a little sorry about it. Not that I'm sorry about Rokhsar's brother—and yet in a way I am. If only I had at least said to him, that day, "Kayumars is a nice name." I do believe he thought I was putting him on. But if I'd only said this, he wouldn't think so. Even now perhaps I ought to pick up the phone and call him. Not for any special reason, you understand, but merely to tell him I wasn't making fun of him.

Kayumars isn't a bad name for a boy, but I'll never call a child of mine Kiki. It's real silly. If I have a daughter like myself, I'll name her Susk. I've only just now thought of it. It's a wonderful choice: anyone who wants can call her Black Susk.* Moreover, Mama is bound to be pleased because it too begins with an S.

---

* The point of the final few lines will be understood in the light of what has been said, earlier in the story, about names and nicknames in the family. The additional feature here is that the name she proposes to inflict on her future daughter means "roach," so the appendage of "black" is even more appropriate than when applied to her own name, "Rose." Of course, her wild idea could hardly be carried into effect in reality.

The Interview

I should tell you, I'm fed to the teeth with the seaside. I didn't want to go last year either, but they forced me to. They wanted to do the same this year, with the additional pretext that Uncle Hosain's kids are coming back to Iran for the summer, and will be going to the seaside also. I can't *stand* their son Hormoz, and I certainly can't stand the seaside. I put my foot down and said I wouldn't go.

Mama said, "Where *do* you want to go, then?"

I replied, "Nowhere. Do I absolutely have to go somewhere?"

Uncle Ardeshir chipped in, "Of course, obviously. So you want to stay in Tehran?" And he said it in such a way as to imply that staying in Tehran was utterly impossible.

"Yes, I do," I said. "I've got things to do."

At this time Uncle Hosain made his point: "Tut! Tut! Tut! You have to do a make-up at school, do you? You lazybones!"

If Mama hadn't been there, I'd have said "yes" and left it at that. But Mama was immediately wounded in her pride: "Make-up?! What nonsense! As if she didn't have anything better to do!"

I prayed fervently that the matter would end here, and that Mama wouldn't continue showing off. But no! She had to say, "You know so little about your own brother's child that you're unaware she's the top student in her class?"

Whenever Mama talks this way, I long to do something to stop being top student.

Uncle Hosain did his fine gentleman act. He neither offered ecstatic praise nor assumed the incredulous expression which people do in such circumstances. After all, people tend not to believe such things, but it's no big deal. In their hearts they say, "You know what these parents are like..." And again, if they do believe it, they think what a stupid dummy a kid must be to have become top student. But you can't explain these things to Mama. Not that I haven't tried to do so: I have, but it didn't work. On one occasion I said to her, "Oh Mama, why do you have to tell everybody? No one believes it." Mama pondered the matter, and stupid me thought she was in agreement. But you know what happened later? Every time she said to someone, "My daughter is first in her class," she would go and get my report-card and show it to them. Just imagine what embarrassments one has to put up with!

This lousy top-student business, once you're outside the four walls of the classroom, is just a big joke. The only good thing about it is that

55

you don't have to put up with the constant harping-on of parents who were top students themselves. Have you ever noticed that *all* parents were top students in their time? It's the same thing with teachers too.

Anyway, whenever Mama puts on this sort of production, I start fiddling with my fingernails and Big Brother starts whistling. On this occasion Uncle Hosain said, "Bravo, my girl! I'll buy you something as a reward. How about a watch?"

At this, Mama asked me, "Didn't Uncle Ardeshir give you a watch this year?"

"*This* year?" I retorted. "It must be six years straight now that I've been getting a watch from him every year."

Uncle Hosain burst out laughing and Uncle Ardeshir gave me a nasty look. But Mama said, "Are you always going to be cadging from your Uncle, you shameless hussy? After all, like a lot of people, he didn't realize you were the top student."

Poor little Uncle Hosain! It was obvious from the beginning that until Mama had hit him over the head with the information, he wouldn't have lifted a finger. I felt so sorry for him that I'd have done anything he asked—except going up north to the seaside.

Finally, Uncle Hosain contrived to get himself off the hook and turned to me: "O.K., so you want to stay in Tehran for the summer? To do what? You don't have to study."

"I've told you why. I have things to do."

Now it was Uncle Ardeshir's turn: "What sort of things, for example?"

Why can't someone just tell this Uncle Ardeshir, "For heaven's sake, go and buy that watch! It's none of your business. Who was talking to you, anyway?" At first I didn't intend to answer him, but he nailed me with such a look that it slipped out, "I want to go and work in an office."

I never thought anything I said would have such an effect. Big Brother stopped whistling, Uncle Hosain started to cough, and Uncle Ardeshir held a match he had lighted for his pipe motionless in mid-air. I waited until he burned his hand, and then reminded him, "Uncle, your match." And last but not least, Mama wailed, "Wha-a-at? What did you say?"

To tell the truth, I wasn't all that serious about the matter. The words just slipped out. And then I wanted to get out of the hassle of going up north with that creep Hormoz and being stared down by

Uncle Ardeshir. However, their reaction forced me to give the matter a serious turn.

With great firmness I stated, "I want to work. An office-job."

Simin's husband's disappointment was complete. And Simin herself cried, as though she were announcing somebody's death, "Did you get that, Amir? Suri wants to work."

He replied, "Must be her belly."

Hadehadeha! Bad taste!

"Stop clowning," Simin said to her husband. "She wants to work in an *office*."

He was not disconcerted: "O.K., let her! Maybe somebody there will be fool enough to take her. These days girls either find a husband on the telephone or they work a duplicator in offices."

I was about to take advantage of his witticisms and quietly slip away but Uncle Ardeshir butted in, "So where are you planning to work?"

Uncle's tough-guy tone will slay you. His name ought to be Flint or James Bond. I wasn't about to back down, so I said, "It's not quite settled yet. Perhaps …"

"Just a minute," piped up Big Brother. "What nonsense is all this? What sort of work can *you* do?"

"I would ask you not to interfere. It's none of your business."

"It's obviously been some time since I kept an eye on you. You're getting very cheeky."

I told him, "Oh, get lost!"

This was too much for Mama: "Suri, you're at it again? Speak politely to your brother."

"Pooh! It's his own fault. He's always poking his nose in. How many hundreds of people do I have to answer to?"

Uncle Ardeshir, to show that I only had to answer to him, intervened and said, "O.K., let her finish and we'll see what she has to say."

"I have nothing more to say. I want to work. That's it!"

Mama pleaded, "But why, my dear? If you're short of pocket-money…"

I repeated, "No. I wanna work! Why can't you understand? What's wrong with that?" I think I must've been speaking very earnestly—my dander was up too—because nobody said a word, but they all merely looked at me in amazement.

Old Khanom Jan spoke up, "All right. She wants to do something interesting for the summer. The poor child is unhappy. How long can

you expect her to hang around with us old fogies? It's not good for her."
Then she turned to me: "Come and sit with me, dearie."

I swear, my dear Khanom Jan's insight is way beyond all these others.'

Big Brother made his contribution, "After all, this creature has absolutely no experience—no skills at all. If her nose starts to run, somebody else will have to wipe it for her."

I totally ignored him.

But Maliheh came to my defense, "She knows all sorts of things. She is in no way inferior to any boy of her age!"

Dear old Maliheh! Whatever she says, it always comes down ultimately to equal rights as between men and women. After all, she's one of those liberated women. There was a picture of them in *Woman Today*. Did you see it? It was enough to make you bust a gut laughing. They were all standing round a pressure cooker full of bean-pilaf, and they had all dipped their spoons into it and were looking at the camera. Posed like those pictures, taken after the decree removing the veil, which can be found in Khanom Jan's album.* In particular there is one picture in her album which, I swear, would fit right into *Woman Today*. The only difference being that in place of the pressure cooker they are grouped around a copper dinner pail and, oh!, there's also a samovar.

Uncle Ardeshir interjected sarcastically, "The lady hasn't yet deigned to inform us where she proposes to work."

It's no use. You just have to answer Uncle. Thank God, I suddenly remembered how Mehri was saying that Mrs. Hosaini was looking for a few good students to assist the teachers in correcting the papers of the junior classes and the Elementary Sixth.

And so I replied, "I propose to mark exam papers. Mrs. Hosaini wants me to." For the moment nobody could make up their mind whether this job in particular was beneath the family honor or not. They all looked expectantly at Uncle Ardeshir. However, he is always opposed to any suggestion which hasn't occurred to him first. This is his historical mission.

He finally passed judgment, "No! You already read and write enough—indeed, more than is good for you. Your eyes will get weak, my girl—and then what? No! This job is totally unsuitable. Now, if there

---

* At Reza Shah's urging, the final decree was promulgated in January 1936.

were some sort of employment that didn't demand too much or give too much trouble…"

Uncle Hosain put in his two-cents'-worth, "Quite right. For example, the Oil Company, the Planning Organization…"

Uncle Ardeshir cut him off, "Yes, yes. Or, for example…"

Before I rightly understood what was happening, he was on the phone talking to a certain "Hasan, my dear chap … ." He kept on speaking of "my niece" and burbling away about the Minister and the Ministry and an interview—and so on and so forth. I was about to ask what the word "interview" meant, but then I thought that he'd turn nasty and start blustering, so I held my tongue.

In short, the business had stupidly become inflated beyond all measure, and however much I tried to gloss it over, it wouldn't work. For one moment it even crossed my mind to go up north with them after all, but matters had gone too far and there was no way back. When Uncle Ardeshir's phone conversation was finished, he barked, "Monday morning you go to the Ministry. Hasan will get an appointment for you with the Minister. 10 a.m. They'll give you a short interview. And make sure you go looking spick-and-span. Do something about that untidy hair of yours."

All I could say was, "Who's Hasan?"

"Hasan Paknehad."

I got it now. That character who parts his hair in the middle and gives off a strong whiff of green cologne, and also has a carbuncle shining on one temple. He's always in and out of Uncle's house. Mama can't stand him. Simin's husband too gives him a very bad name. I said, "Well, Uncle …"

However, Uncle wasn't listening and began to speak of the Minister. "We were at the American College together. Dr. Jordan, God rest his soul…"

I was no longer tuned in. I've heard stories of Dr. Jordan (God rest his soul!) at least once a week from Uncle Ardeshir for ages. I waited until he would finish in the hope of persuading him that I needn't go to see the Minister after all. But in vain. I should've known from the start that stories of the late Dr. Jordan never end and that there is no way of persuading Uncle Ardeshir, especially in such matters. He always says that such things teach you how to deal with life. I've already told you about the business of the Chief Archivist. Oh well … That's the way Uncle is.

Anyhow, this is how the whole affair started. Now just listen, and I'll tell you the rest of it.

On Monday morning Simin turned up at the crack of dawn, put my hair straight and smartened me up. I kept saying, "I'm not supposed to be going to a wedding," but nobody paid any attention.

Mama said sharply, "It's not a question of that. Your Uncle's reputation is involved here."

For God's sake! Just think what sort of things my Uncle's reputation depends on!

Whenever I put my hair up, I have to laugh at my own appearance. In the first place, my hair feels heavy on my head. Secondly, my neck bobs around in my collar like that of a goose. However, my appearance isn't all that important. I went to the Ministry, "on the dot of 10." That's an expression I learned at the Ministry—I hadn't known it before. Well, when I got there, the Chief of Staff to the Minister (one always has to go first to the Minister's Chief of Staff) said on the telephone, "Someone has come, sir, and claims to have an appointment with Your Excellency on the dot of 10." He'd never have thought of this way of speaking himself—he was a real drip, you can't imagine. When he was speaking to me, you would have thought he was Alain Delon.* Mehri should've been there. She surely would've fallen for him.

The Minister said something or other. No doubt he asked, "A woman or a man?" because Alain Delon said, "It's a lady, sir."

Once again the Minister must have said something, for Alain Delon replied, "Permit me to ask." He looked languidly in my direction and asked, "Who exactly sent you?"

Obviously the Minister had asked him this, so I said, "Uncle Ardeshir, that is to say Mr. Paknehad."

He addressed the telephone once more. "Her uncle, Mr. Paknehad, sir ... Very good, sir."

I tried to set matters straight: "No, Mr. Paknehad is ..."

But he wouldn't listen. He replaced the receiver: "The room of the Secretary to His Excellency the Minister. He'll direct you." Then he went back to work as though I didn't exist. I was really furious, because he knew perfectly well that I was still there. Phony Alain Delon!

Well now, if the Chief of Staff was an Alain Delon, the Secretary was as skinny as Twiggy.** He wore his hair shorter than the Chief of Staff.

---

* Alain Delon: heartthrob French actor of the time.

** Twiggy: British fashion model of the period, the earliest representative of the anorexic female figure.

All around his eyes he had worked on his lashes—to make them longer—just as Homa does. And I don't know what he had rubbed on his face to give it such a yoghurty color. "I'd like to see the Minister," I said boldly. "GGGot an appointment, deawie?" He spoke in a peculiar manner. He pronounced his G's with three or four times the normal emphasis. His R was something between a normal R and a W. In short, he spoke like a Westerner trying to speak Persian. "I certainly do!" I replied.

From his manner it was obvious that I was making a big nuisance of myself. He looked at me narrowly out of his made-up eyes. "I don't have a note of this. Go to the Chief of Staff ..."

"I was just there."

For a moment he chewed fiercely on his gum and said in a rage, "That door there!"

When I got to the door of that room I turned round to make sure which door he meant. I caught Twiggy nodding with his head to a certain female sitting in his room, who looked like nothing in particular. His eyes were saying, "Get a load of this one!" I, for my part, was saying under my breath, "Yeah, get a load of me!" But I was plenty mad at this Secretary.

To tell you the truth, I felt like getting out of there, but there was a guard standing at the end of the hallway, and for some reason I felt that if I started to walk out he'd stop me.

The Minister's door was ajar, and I peeped in through the opening. All I could see were two leather chairs and an oversized table, covered in green baize like a billiard table, with chairs arranged around it. The guard was looking the other way and I was about to leave, but a nondescript attendant, also standing in the corridor, motioned to me to enter. From his impatient manner it was clear that I mustn't thwart him.

I knocked softly. A very loud voice said at that moment, "So what's happened to this 'Armstrong?'"

I imagined that this term must be some sort of password. Once inside, I realized that the Minister was speaking on the telephone. He had his back to the door, and I was about to leave again, but the Minister turned his swivel chair in my direction. His eyes were blazing with anger. I couldn't make out whether this was because I had come in, or because I was about to go out again. At first I shifted from one foot to the other, but then I made up my mind to leave. However, just as I made to do so, the Minister indicated that I should stay and also close the door. I did it in such a way as to suggest that I was intending to do so anyway. The Minister's next remark on the telephone was, "Yes, right away." He held on to the receiver while looking me up and down. I felt my arms growing longer and didn't know what to do with them.

His Excellency looked deeply into my eyes and said in careful English, "GOOD MORNING!"

Quickly, I also said, "GOOD MORNING!"

When Uncle Ardeshir announced that I was to be interviewed, fool that I was, I should have realized that the idea was to test my English. But I hadn't grasped this point, and I now went completely to pieces.

The Minister, still staring into my eyes, went on, "HOW ARE YOU?"

My own "T'ANK YOU!" clashed with the Minister's words "Mr. Armstrong," and I realized that he was now speaking to Mr. Armstrong personally. It was a disaster, and I could've died with embarrasment. Unfortunately, I had no way of escape. On one side there were the attendant, the Secretary, the Chief of Staff and the guard, on the other the Minister was sitting staring at me from behind his glasses. I was in a real fix. The Minister laughed, and I didn't know whether it was at me or Mr. Armstrong. However, I resolved not to be discomfited and to attribute to Mr. Armstrong whatever subsequently developed.

The Minister: "YES, YES."

Then silence.

Then again: "YES."

Silence again. Loud laughter.

Again: "YES, OH YES."

Silence. Very serious: "YES, OF COURSE, YES."

A very, very long silence.

And then: "SEE YOU TONIGHT. GOOD-BYE."

I understood everything he said but I didn't get the chance to feel good about that. Especially since my ability to speak English had forsaken me at a bad moment, and I was bathed in sweat from embarrassment.

The Minister now turned away from me and I drew a breath of relief and leaned against the wall, regarding him more calmly. That is to say, what I looked at was the back of his head, which was red and had two folds of flesh. It was exactly like a string of beef-sausages—you must've seen them—which they sell in the *Iran Super*. The Minister gave an order: "Come here!"

I stood motionless, wondering whether he meant me or not, since he still had his back to me, and I was lost in the folds at the back of his noggin. He now turned back to face me. As I had been looking at his folds, my eyes were directed straight ahead and met his full on. I was completely taken unawares, and lowered my head. My arms grew even longer.

The Minister addressed me: "I'm with you now, my dear. Come up closer and let me look at you."

I went forward, but you can't imagine in what a fashion. First my arms went one meter ahead, then my trunk and finally my legs. When I got to the desk, I had no idea what to do.

The Minister invited me, "Sit down and let's see."

I practically hurled myself onto a leather chair. It looked firm enough, but I sank into it like a clumsy porpoise. You can't imagine what it cost me to straighten myself out.

The Minister began, "So, Paknehad is your uncle, eh? Well, well, the old scoundrel never told me he had a niece—let alone such a nice-looking one!"

I cried out, "No, Mr. Paknehad is …" I tried to slip in a "sir" like the Chief of Staff, but my tongue wouldn't do my bidding and I ended up sticking it out.

"I understand, I understand, ha-ha-ha …"

I didn't understand just what he understood, and by the time I got to asking, the attendant I mentioned as being in the corridor now came in and stood by the door like a wooden post.

The Minister barked, "Tea!"

The attendant bowed, and I tried not to laugh, because I had thought that this sort of thing had gone out of fashion.

However, the Minister started again, "Now tell me and let's see…" As I started to ask what I should say, the phone rang.

The Minister said, "Tell 'em I've gone to the Prime Minister's office." He put the phone down again and turned to me. "Well, so you were saying …"

Before I could ask what I was supposed to say, there was a knock at the door and Alain Delon entered with some papers. His way of walking was something to behold, for he advanced exactly as though he were on springs.

The Minister growled, "Put 'em on the table!"

Alain Delon placed one hand behind his back, bent forward and whispered something in his chief's ear. The Minister started to sign the documents as Alain Delon smoothed them out for him one by one and placed them before him.

Once again the telephone rang and His Excellency answered, "Who? Yes, yes, speaking ..."

He held the receiver to one side, straightened up the papers for Alain Delon, who now picked them up and inquired, "Will there be anything else, sir?"

But he received no answer. I deliberately cleared my throat so that he should realize I was aware of his discomfiture. He was thoroughly down in the mouth. D'you know how I realized that he was particularly upset? As he was leaving, he forgot to walk on springs. I said to myself, "He's a really changed man."

His Excellency was on the telephone again: "Is the speech ready? ... Good ... What about the translation of it? ... Send it over for me to see. Have you fixed up the schedule for the trip? ... No, no! Cancel it! I have business for two days in Venice ... 8 a.m. the day after tomorrow. O.K."

That conversation was over. Twiggy came in and left. Then the phone rang again.

The Minister answered, "Tell them I have to go to a committee meeting. And I don't want to be disturbed by anybody for the next few minutes."

Once more he replaced the receiver and the attendant brought the tea. I went to squeeze my lemon, and a squirt of juice shot into my eye. I went to wipe my eye and my tea nearly tipped over.

"Do you like rum?" His Excellency asked.

He'd finally found the time to speak to me. With one eye closed I replied, "I've never been to Rome."

At this he really laughed aloud: "Not the city of Rome—rum, my dear, like this.* A drop of it in tea is quite delicious. I take it for my grippe. Would *you* like some?"

I really must've been born to be put down. I simply said, "Thank you, no."

My eye was killing me. I got out my handkerchief and put it against it. I do believe that His Excellency thought because I had made a gaffe I was crying, and he made to say that it wasn't important. Indeed, he

---

* The confusion arises partly from Suri's lack of sophistication, but also because the two words ("rum" and "Rome") are written and pronounced identically in Persian.

said to me in a very kind way, "As it happens, I'm about to go to Rome— would you like to come with me?"

I poured all the astonishment that was in the eye covered by the handkerchief, into my uncovered eye and looked firmly at the Minister.

He went on, "It's only for a week."

I can't tell you how confused I was. Somehow or other I stammered out, "O.K., I'll take a drop."

This time His Excellency really did show sympathy for me. He asked compassionately, "How old are you?"

"I'm seventeen." If Mama had been there, she would've said like a shot, "Sixteen and four months." Good thing she wasn't there, because it was clear that the Minister wasn't too happy even with seventeen. He put his head on one side, looked at me and said, "So you're a Lolita ..."

"No," I answered, "my name is Suri." Lolita is even worse than Suri—at least for someone who looks like me.

He laughed. Obviously I had put my foot in it again and had missed the point. But anyway, it was evident from his laugh that if he couldn't forgive all my other booboos, at least he did forgive my youth.

He continued, "So your name is Suri? No doubt in the house of that uncle of yours they call you Susu."

Susu?! Good grief! I was ready to throw up. Now I was ready to put him in the wrong and say, "No. What they call me is Black Suri," but I didn't say it. For no particular reason I was reminded of Kayumars, no doubt because they call him Kiki. His Excellency peered into my face and I came over all hot. Recently, whenever I think of Kayumars, I feel like this. I can't think why.

The Minister said, "Oh dear! You're blushing, my little Susu."

Whenever I come over hot, I turn the color of a boiled beet. You can't imagine what a disgrace it all is.

At times the Minister's speech seemed to suffer an impediment, at others he produced a whistling sound: his pronounciation of "Susu" was absolutely ridiculous, and I was seized with a fit of laughter. To prevent myself laughing, I busied myself with a lock of hair which had come loose. I pushed it up behind my ear. In this way, I both stopped myself laughing and saved Uncle from losing face.

His Excellency smiled. "Leave your hair alone—it looks nice as it is."

I went, "Er ... hum." I couldn't think of anything except this lousy "Er ... hum," and inwardly I cursed myself for not asking Uncle exactly what "interview" meant.

Now he stood up behind his desk and leaned forward on it. "Very well, Susu: so what sort of work do you fancy doing?"

I replied, "I don't know—this is the first time I've had the idea of doing such things."

Once again, he chuckled loudly. You can't imagine what a pleasant laugh it was. The only bad thing about it was that I didn't understand what he was laughing at, and I felt intimidated.

"What sort of things do you mean, you little devil?"

I remembered Big Brother's words and said abruptly, "I've absolutely no experience. If you don't think I'd be suitable ..."

"OH DARLING ...!"

I went on sharply, "I don't know English. To tell the truth, I don't have any real skills at all. Uncle wasted his time telling me to come here."

The Minister countered, "Paknehad was quite right to send you to me. And like a good girl you must say to him, 'Thank you, Uncle.'"

"Mr. Paknehad is *not* my uncle. I'm the niece of Ardeshir Mirza."

The Minister's smile froze on his face, and he adjusted his glasses and looked me up and down. This time he looked at me as though I had made a poor joke: "Ardeshir Mirza? Who's Ardeshir Mirza?!"

"One of your classmates—from the American College."

The Minister stood up straight, pulled down his jacket, took a step back and looked at me this time as though he had never seen me before. He moved his neck around inside his collar, and I almost thought that the starch in it would add another line to those already at the back of his head.

I looked straight at him and said, "Umph!"

This time it was the Minister who began to stammer, "But it was you ... you said ..."

I replied, "I didn't say anything—Alain Delon, I mean your Chief of Staff, made the mistake. He wouldn't listen to a word I said." I particularly wanted to complain some more about that Chief of Staff, but I saw that the Minister was waiting to hear what mistake had been made. So I continued: "Mr. Paknehad is a friend of Uncle Ardeshir. He telephoned in the hope that you could give me a job." I was hoping to work in the word "interview" somewhere, but was afraid of getting it wrong.

At this the Minister said, "A job ...? Ah, yes ... er ... a job ... quite right, a job ..."

I can't imagine why he had suddenly become so flustered. I was about to say that the matter of a job wasn't again all that important, but by the time I got to "job," he was already speaking again: "At present we do not have suitable employment for you in the Ministry. I very much regret. Of course, it's merely that … I will telephone Mr. Ardeshir Mirza myself … However, now I must attend to my duties. Alas, in a few minutes I have a committee meeting, and then … er … I have to see the Prime Minister."

I remained sitting there because I didn't know what I was supposed to do. Above all, I didn't know what to do with my long arms.

The Minister said, "Very well … On your way home now?"

I tried to speak in a very well-bred, literary manner so that he'd be sorry not to have offered me a job. "Yes, indeed. I shall proceed to my place of residence."*

He couldn't have heard the last syllable because by that time I was already in the corridor.

∞ ∞ ∞

This year, once again, we're going up north.

---

* The Minister's final remark to her is so flat in style as to be almost rude, but her retaliatory use of high-flown language is particularly inappropriate in Persian, since it should not be employed in speaking of oneself.

Peyton Place*

On Saturday evening our Mama and the rest were invited to the home of Erfaq od-Dowleh's son-in-law. As for me, I thought I'd sit down and work out my algebra problems, and then have a look at *Peyton Place* on the T.V. The fact is that until that evening I had never even seen it. For God's sake don't mention that to Mehri—not that it's a big deal! But all the rest of them talk about "Betty" and "Allison" as if they'd grown up together. One Sunday, when the kids had all gotten together to work on trigonometry, just as I was about to study the figure of the problem set, Mehri suddenly said to Homa, "Allison's grown a bit thin, don't you think?"

"No. Since she's had her hair cut shorter, she just seems to be skinny."

Rokhsar chipped in, "She made a mistake having it cut short. It doesn't suit her."

Homa: "I think she looks more elegant, much nicer than Betty."

If I hadn't grumbled about getting on with the trigonometry, they'd have gone on arguing forever about the beauty of Betty and Allison respectively. Anyway, when this bunch start talking that way, you don't have the nerve to say you haven't a clue about it all. It's not just Mehri and the girls, either: in our house and at Simin's place, and everybody else's, there's constant talk of *Peyton Place*. Even Amir, Simin's husband, is prepared to ignore the show only when he's playing poker. Simin herself is a pathetic case: if she misses a program, she's as miserable as a dog for two or three days, and telephones four or five friends to ask how far along the action has moved. And do you think she's satisfied, even then? No! She feels she's been permanently deprived of various bits of the plot. And then there's the case of Maliheh. Whenever there's talk of television, she starts to pooh-pooh. "Who on earth looks at television?" she keeps saying. Yet just a few days ago—I can't remember how it happened—Simin had missed the program, and there was Maliheh busy giving her a detailed account of the whole story. I arrived just as she was saying, "Then Rodney gave Betty a kiss … "

---

* The much-vaunted, titillating novel by Grace Metalious (1956), which became the basis for a soap-opera series, immensely popular both in the U.S.A. and internationally.

Simin replied, "Bless my soul! Kissed her, you say? The wife he'd divorced!"

But Maliheh's "Oh well!" was meant to imply, "You're really out of touch!"

Now, whatever situation arises, Simin is always worried she may seem old-fashioned in Maliheh's eyes, so she now felt badly put-down and immediately came back: "But you can't help feeling sorry for Steve, poor devil."

I asked, "So who's this Steve?"

Maliheh started to explain, but I lost all patience: "Maliheh, my girl, you're the one who's always saying you don't watch T.V.!"

Simin interrupted irritably, "Suri, you're making a nuisance of yourself again, aren't you? Ignore her, Maliheh, and tell us the rest. Then what happened? What did Betty do then?"

As though I'd never spoken, or she herself hadn't earlier denied watching television, Maliheh calmly resumed her narrative.

Oh well, forget it! As I started out saying, Mama and the rest were due to go to the home of Erfaq od-Dowleh's son-in-law. The whole family had been invited. For the betrothal evening Erfaq od-Dowleh's family hadn't issued invitations, since it was just before the forty-day mourning period for Grandma was up, and they wanted to have things quiet.* For the same reason, nobody had yet had a really good look at all the new relatives. They were all absolutely dying to give them a proper once-over.

Of course, nothing had happened so far. Everybody had freely pooled whatever they knew about the son-in-law's family. The evening we were at the home of Maliheh's parents—I've told you about that, haven't I?—the talk was of nothing else but this. The primary complaint was that they might've waited till after the forty-day mourning period was finally over.

Maliheh's mother had said her piece: "What's to be done with the young people of this generation, I ask you?! They've no respect for anything! If they'd just waited those few days, what difference would it've made?"

Of course, she had forgotten how anxious she herself had been about getting Maliheh and Big Brother married off. She wouldn't even

---

* Mourning rites are traditionally taken very seriously for religious reasons. Apart from the inappropriateness of other social events in such a situation, heavy demands on time would preclude making arrangements for an engagement party.

wait till Uncle Hosain got back from abroad. At that time, she'd put it this way: "They're young, after all, bless my soul! The world belongs to the young, my dear, and the old ones must be wise enough to go along with what they want."

Auntie Fakhri disagreed: "Their elders are to blame. Look! Showkat—for heaven's sake!—is a young girl: was she likely to be left on your hands? And Parvaneh—God bless her!—is both beautiful and rich. If one husband doesn't work out, there'll be plenty more." You see how it goes, for crying out loud? This same Auntie Fakhri, when they found that crummy suitor for me (don't tell anyone, will you!), kept declaring, "I must say, he's a fine boy. These days husbands are hard to find. There are girls looking like a million bucks, but they have to sit at home eating their hearts out for a husband."

Mama got annoyed at this. "Really, Fakhri, my daughter's not exactly deformed, nor is she a beggar. But, thank the Lord!, *she*'s not eating her heart out for a husband. It's no time to talk of such matters now."

It was a good thing that Mama voiced her indignation. Otherwise, I might've become the subject of a long rigmarole by the family, not to rule out the possibility of that pathetic little man also becoming entangled with me. Anyway, what I wanted to speak about was Parvaneh and her husband. Uncle Hosain asked Big Brother, "How's Erfaq od-Dowleh's business doing?"

"I don't really know," he replied. "But Parvaneh herself is a very nice girl, and pretty too." I thought he blushed a bit here.

You can't imagine what a look Maliheh gave him. After all, before he married her, it was understood he would wed Parvaneh. What I think happened was that when Erfaq od-Dowleh's estates were seized, the relatives closer to hand changed Big Brother's mind for him.

Uncle Ardeshir now piped up, "If you ask me, sir, Erfaq od-Dowleh doesn't have that much left by now. That's why he practically gave his daughter away to this fellow."

Uncle Hosain inquired, "Is the son-in-law doing well, then?"

"Boundless wealth, my dear sir. Immense. Before the War, his father was a young ragamuffin without a shirt to his back, but during the war years he got into tires, and now there's money, money—my dear sir!—money beyond counting."

Uncle Hosain again: "True enough. I know him well. But I hope the undertaker robs him of it in the end! Look! His wife was dying, but although everybody kept telling him to send her to Europe for treatment, he wouldn't even hear of it for fear of having to spend a penny or two. He argued that our own doctors are good enough."

I asked, "Did his wife die, then, Uncle?"

"No, she's still alive, and strong as a bear."

I was about to say, "So he wasn't so far wrong, then," but Fati, Uncle Hosain's wife (who herself goes to Europe once a month for a so-called "check-up"), intervened: "The point was to show how stingy the man must be."

I retorted, "I imagined the point was that his wife should get treatment." But nobody paid me any attention, and Uncle Hosain came out with "I've a better idea: let them give the money to me ..."

Auntie Fakhri had her answer ready: "So that, within a couple of days, you could flush it away down the toilet, I suppose?"

He pretended not to hear. (You'd never believe how good our family are at not listening to what others are saying.) Instead, he continued his musings, "I once saw a villa in Nice ... "

Simin's husband had to say his piece: "Before you ever got to Nice, you'd have gambled away the price of the villa in Monte Carlo. Come on, let them give the money to me!"

Simin, quick as a flash, "Yeah! To go chasing loose women with!"

"Chasing loose women? What—me?! That God should hear you say such a thing!"

Now it was Auntie Fakhri's turn: "You young kids don't know the value of money. When I was a child ... "

"Auntie dear," Simin's husband cut in, "you're still a child, still a young thing, still bright and shining!"

At this, Auntie gave one of those cackles that put me in mind of her screechings on the last day of the mourning ceremonies for Grandma. Finally she said, "Bless my soul! You're a real charmer, I must say."

I turned on Amir: "Shall I say it? Shall I tell what you used to say about Auntie Fakhri's youth and beauty?"

Auntie said, "Say it! I'd love to hear it! Tell us what he used to say."

Simin gave me an angry look, and Mama too bit her lip in disapproval. Simin's husband then said, "Auntie dear, you were speaking of money," making at the same time a menacing gesture at me.

Auntie replied, "That's right. If I had all that money ... "

At which Uncle Hasan whispered to Maliheh's father, "She'd bury it all in the garden." The latter started to laugh, but noticed his wife and changed it to a clearing of the throat, so that Uncle Hasan was obliged to laugh solo.

Maliheh's mother gave her husband a black look and said to Uncle Hasan, "Were you with me, dear? I say, a man ought not to have all that money—bless my soul!— nor a tire-dealer for a daddy. Now, if Erfaq od-Dowleh had given his daughter to some penniless prince or other, my dear, what would've been wrong with that?"

Simin's husband retorted, "It wouldn't have been wrong, but nor would it have made that much difference, madam. It's just that at this moment we would have been taking the penniless prince apart instead. We'd be saying, 'Curse the worthless fellow for wasting all his ancestral wealth!'"

These words were both to the point and amusing. But Uncle Ardeshir gave nobody the chance to confirm them or even to laugh. Instead, he came in with a contribution of his own: "Of course ... But one might make an objection, my dear sir: after all, penury is not a virtue. What I *would* say is, one should not try to acquire wealth by any and every means and at any price whatsoever. Apart from that, money's a very fine thing, provided one grows rich in an honorable way—let him be a porter, let him do street-cleaning, sir!"

Uncle really does say such stupid things sometimes that it makes you nauseous. After all, for God's sake, have you ever heard of a porter or a street-sweeper getting rich by their trades? Such activities may well be honorable enough, but tell me, have you ever heard of such a thing?

Khanom Jan spoke up now. "Anyway, God grant the girl good fortune, my dears! The rest is just an extra."

Everybody turned to nod an indication of agreement with Khanom Jan's words, but Uncle Ardeshir thought otherwise. "That's just talk, Khanom Jan. The girl was married off for money—and money doesn't bring happiness, you know."

All the noggins suddenly came to a stop in the midst of their agreement with Khanom Jan, and now enthusiastically began to wag in support of Uncle.

Khanom Jan was not to be put down: "Be grateful you've never known what it means to be penniless. If you had, my friends, you'd soon realize what things money can bring. Health, education, comfort—and happiness too. Of course it can bring that, my friend!"

With Khanom Jan, even when she says things you dearly wish were not true, when you think about them, you soon see that they are. But with Uncle, it's the opposite: even his valid remarks tend to appear false. That is to say, his statements are like the content of an exercise in composition-style. What I'm trying to say is that even if they are valid, they're so flat and insipid that you are thoroughly turned off. Take the above remark of his, "Money doesn't bring happiness." How many times do you think I've copied that one out in class, eh? And what a desperate struggle it takes each time to affirm that money doesn't bring happiness! If they give me this assignment again this year, I'll incorporate Khanom Jan's remarks. I mightn't get a good grade—but so what?

I thought that after what Khanom Jan had said, Uncle Ardeshir might pipe down. Not a bit of it! He even raised his voice a notch: "You're not in touch with the situation, Khanom Jan. A young girl like her has to love the fellow. What would she do with money?"

Now it was my turn: "How do you know Parvaneh doesn't love her husband?"

Maliheh's mother raised one eyebrow and Auntie Fakhri gave me the sort of look that said, "You see, God preserve us! The girls of this generation are utterly shameless, my dears."

Uncle countered with "Pardon?"

That's another of Uncle's special tricks. Whenever he cannot immediately think of a crushing reply, or when he is unable to put his adversary down with an "I would venture to say" or "You don't understand at all," he simply pretends not to have heard the other person's words. Yet he asks "What did you say?" with such a contemptuous air as to suggest "I didn't catch it, but the nonsense you uttered is not worth repeating anyway!" As for me, however, having long since taken the measure of my uncle, I was on this occasion in no way disconcerted: in a very deliberate tone I repeated, "I said: How do you know that Parvaneh doesn't love … ?"

But Big Brother now jumped into the middle of my remarks: "And how do *you* know she does love him, Miss Big-Chief Meddler?"

Answering Big Brother always boils down to saying something like "Yeah, yeah, and you too!" As a matter of fact, most of the time I don't bother to answer him at all, but on this occasion my dander was up and I blurted out: "I know because Parvaneh herself told me. She said they're both in love …"

To tell the truth, I hadn't seen Parvaneh since the holiday. And when I do see her, we don't have much to say to each other, anyway. I didn't really have the faintest idea whether she loved her husband or not. It was just that this bunch were all talking as though, simply because the boy's daddy was in the tire-business, the girl could not possibly love him. They didn't speak a blind word about the bridegroom himself for one to get some idea what sort of a person he was.

There they were, talking a blue streak and pooh-poohing away to give the impression that his daddy was an utter nonperson. This bunch, all so proud of their papas and mamas, haven't done a thing to maintain their name, their social status, or their wealth. They all cheat each other, but if someone with no background does the same thing and becomes wealthy, they get up in arms and seem to imagine he has stolen their patrimonial inheritance. After all, Erfaq od-Dowleh's son-in-law was not himself in the tire-business—it was his daddy. And then again, what's wrong with selling tires? You understand what I mean? I don't really get it, but I do know that in our family whenever they want to badmouth somebody they say, "He got into selling tires after the War." What does this lot do themselves that selling tires seems so terrible to them?! You'd think they're all sitting there making great scientific discoveries and working for the good of humanity—good grief!

But you can't say such things, so I didn't say them. Anyway, what I had already said was remarkable enough to shut Uncle's mouth for a few moments. It also annoyed Big Brother. Undoubtedly, the reason for this was that he was bound to expect Parvaneh to shed tears till her dying day at parting from him, and never again fall in love with anyone else. The fellow himself marries and goes his own way, yet he still expects the girl to linger in bitter disappointment at home. Now let Maliheh dare to breathe a word about the equal rights of men and women!

Still, forget it! I was speaking of Parvaneh and her husband. I felt really uneasy that he might not amount to much and she wouldn't be able to love him at all.

Simin asked, "Is that true, Suri? She told you herself?" It was obvious that she longed for me to have told the truth, so that for a few days to come she could taunt her husband with tales of Parvaneh and her husband's lovey-dovey billing and cooing. You can't imagine just how *romantic* Simin is, and how upset she gets that Amir is absolutely not the least bit so. When Richard Burton married Elizabeth Taylor, Simin wouldn't speak to Amir for a whole week.

Maliheh had her eyes glued on Big Brother to see what he would say.

He offered her a forced smile, which only made her more anxious, and said to Simin, "The kid's talking nonsense. Don't you know her yet? How on earth can *she* understand what love and lovemaking's all about?"

But Simin's husband chipped in, "She knows about one thing better than you and I do. If you keep talking in front of her about this one and that one getting married, the girl will get all worked up. Mother, why don't you give some thought to marrying off Suri?"

Mama eyed Amir narrowly, so he went on, "O.K. Let's talk a bit about our little baby doll ... "

Ha-ha-ha. Big joke.

Simin's husband protested, "I'm serious ... "

Uncle Hasan countered, "Is that possible?"

This time it was my turn to laugh.

Simin's husband: "Didn't I say so? As soon as we talk of baby-dolls, she starts to titter. Mother dear, Parvaneh's husband has a younger brother. It wouldn't be a bad idea to fix Suri up with *him*."

Mama now asked, "Really?" Up till then she hadn't said a word—get me?

Amir replied, "Believe me, ma'am."

Uncle Ardeshir puffed his pipe vigorously a couple of times. "Is that so? I wasn't aware of that. What sort of a lad is he?"

Amir answered, "Cut from the same cloth, sir. Been to the West. Properly educated." Then he nodded at me for Uncle Hosain's benefit and winked. You can imagine I was listening most carefully. This really made me mad.

Then he added, "There she goes! From now until Friday night, she'll be dreaming of his good looks."

Simin blurted out, "Oh dear! Are we entertaining on Saturday? What about *Peyton Place*?"

At this point I turned to Amir: "You're always burbling, talk away to all eternity. I'm not due to go anywhere on Saturday night."

"Very well. I'll say no more. It's a small price to pay. Don't worry, they'll take you too."

Simin, plaintively to Mama, "Can't we change the day?"

I retorted angrily, "I'll be taken? Forget it. I'm *not* going."

Big Brother added his bit, "You and your big mouth."

"It's better than yours!"

Uncle Ardeshir now tried to persuade me: "You're invited too, madam."

I rejoined, "Mama, didn't Uncle say I didn't have to go, and you agreed?"

"Ah, well ... Just a minute, let me see what Amir has to say. Amir, how old is he? What does he do?"

I insisted, "I'm *not* going *anywhere* on Saturday."

Big Brother shouted, "To hell with you! What a pain in the neck you are, you stupid little brat!"

At this point Simin addressed the whole group, "Can't we change the day?"

Once again, nobody replied. It was obvious that the movie about the family of Erfaq od-Dowleh's son-in-law was much more interesting than *Peyton Place*. Indeed, if they were to make a film like *Peyton Place* about *our* family, the original *Peyton Place* wouldn't stand a chance.

But stand a chance or not, I intended to sit on my butt on Saturday, and after solving my math problems, to watch *Peyton Place*. But would they let me? There I was busy with my algebra when Mama and Uncle Ardeshir came into my room and bugged me to get dressed and go along with them. I huffed and puffed but to no avail.

I protested, "I've got homework to do. I'm not coming."

Uncle tried to be firm. "Don't talk rubbish, dear! The radio has announced that because of heavy snow, all schools are closed. Get up and get ready!" He didn't even wait for an answer, but went downstairs to instruct Ali Aqa to put on the snow chains and park Uncle's own car in the yard. (Uncle still doesn't know how to drive through an eight-meter wide gateway.)

I was so miffed I couldn't even enjoy the idea of a school holiday. Mama too wasn't to be put off, but immediately opened my wardrobe door and laid out my dark-blue velvet dress with my rabbit-skin topcoat.

I kept on resisting: "I'm not wearing those."

"My wardrobe-door is open," Mama coaxed me. "Go and pick out whatever you fancy and put it on. Just be quick, we have to pick up Khanom Jan on the way."

Now, if I myself wanted to go to a party, Mama would never permit me to come near her wardrobe, you understand? But when they propose to *take* me, it's a case of "Go and pick out whatever you fancy!"

I spun it out for a full hour. I dragged out all Mama's clothes, and piled up her earrings and necklaces. But, after all that, I put on my gray woolen sweater, together with my black pants. I also draped my dark shawl around my neck.

The expression on the face of Mama and Uncle, when they caught sight of me, was something to behold. It was just as though the ceiling of the room had come crashing down.

Mama asked, "Couldn't you at least have left your hair unbraided?"

I replied, "Oh well, when it's not done, all hell breaks loose, and Uncle feels disgraced."

Put out at this, Uncle said, "Let's get going, madam. It's no use, no use at all trying to do anything with her."

I was about to say, "Going to a tire merchant's house is no big deal. Now an honorable street sweeper's home, that really is something…" But I slipped on the snow and came a cropper. My little speech was cut short, and my pants got soaking wet through.

∞　∞　∞

And, on top of it all, I never got to see *Peyton Place* after all!

Paikan Place

That day everything was at sixes and sevens. For a start, just as we were ready to leave, it began to snow again—the eighth snowfall of the year. Do you remember what a freeze we had? Our street was up to its waist in snow, even the intersection at the top of the street. Just where Ali Aqa was about to turn the car around, a man was squatting and (in the phrase favored by Mehri's old maid-servant) "dipping his hand into the water"—in this case, of course, dipping it into the *snow*. Uncle Ardeshir immediately looked down his nose and bristled, "Little no-account fellow, doing it on people's streets!"

Of course, what he really meant was, "Doing it on my sister's street!" You must understand that Uncle considers all the land for several kilometers around his own house and those of his various relatives as inherited freehold property. If this wretched little man had been doing his business on another street, it wouldn't have been "people's streets" and Uncle, presumably, would simply have turned away.

Mama scowled disapprovingly, "May he get his just deserts!" To me she said, "Suri, look the other way!"

Ali Aqa tried to turn quickly. He really stepped on the gas, and the car sank heavily into the snowdrifts. However much he revved up, it wouldn't come free. It was stuck in a bad spot, or rather at the very spot where the little man was freely visible to all and sundry. You could see everything, even the yellow stream which passed from him onto the road, and from which steam then ascended. You couldn't help seeing it, whether you wanted to or not. All the time I was thinking, how is he able to do it in such cold weather?

Uncle was still puffing and blowing and boiling with indignation, putting on a show like some rascally panhandler waylaying people on the Tajrish bridge. And Mama was still firmly restraining my curiosity so that I shouldn't turn my head round to see the fellow. My neck was growing stiff. The wheels of the car were spinning like a top, covering the unfortunate wretch in mud and snow and still making no advance. He was an interesting little chap—it's quite impossible to imagine his like: amid all this noise and confusion and mud and mess, he calmly finished his business and stood up again. After he had left, Uncle continued his huffing and puffing for a while and then, at the end of his rope, got out of the car to supervise Ali Aqa's efforts. When we got going again, two clumps of snow had settled, one on the little man's impure leftovers and another on Uncle's hat.

To cut matters short, let's drop this topic. When it snows I'm quite fond of Tehran because it becomes a more agreeable and cleaner city. Don't you think so? Even that square where they park the Paikans, which looks like Kamran Yazdi's candy-store, where they hang lanterns all around—what's it called again? Mehri's lot call it "The Paikan Place": even that looks nice too.*

Another good thing about the snow is that many places one doesn't wish to see will disappear beneath it.

Anyway, as I was saying before, when it snows I like Tehran. I also like driving in the snow, but not together with Mama and Uncle because nothing ever suits them.

There Mama was grumbling again, "This year the winter will never end. We've had a bad time of it. What a winter it's been!"

Uncle rubbed his hands together and said, "No precedent for it in the last twenty-five years, I tell you."

Listening to Uncle, you imagine you're reading a newspaper. Newspapers, when they wish to say that an incident is particularly important, declare either "No precedent for it in the last twenty-five years," or "Unparalleled in the Middle East."

But forget that, too. On the Shemiran highway three cars had collided and were more or less blocking the whole width of the road. I immediately thought, "Good, we're stuck again!" But we didn't get stuck, and I was really disappointed. Uncle started talking about the bad state of the roads: "... these ridiculous highways, these decrepit roads. As far as I'm aware, this country always has hot summers and hard, cold winters, right? But nothing is ever done to match its climate. With one snowfall, the roads are blocked. With one strong bout of sunshine, the asphalt softens up. Life becomes paralyzed, I tell you, totally paralyzed. No one cares a damn, no one thinks of other people. Just their own pockets, my friend, their own pockets."

And yet again, if he doesn't talk exactly like the newspapers, he says things which you can hear all the time around you. Everybody

---

* The name of the present story is in some ways a play on that of the author's other story, *Peyton Place*. The resemblance in Persian is much closer than in English, involving the difference of only *one* letter. The word *paikan* means "arrow/javelin," and refers here to the name of the standard automobile produced in Iran.

talks like this, don't they? That is to say, the only thing they talk about—and they do so with great courage—is the appalling state of the roads. When they get together, they speak of nothing else. You've got to admire the way they can go on and on and on, let's be fair! One Friday, in Khanom Jan's house, they talked about these things at such length that I could've died. After all, the scar left by the lands which the State had seized from Uncle was still fresh, so this matter too was appended to the criticism of the highways. Now, I should add that whenever the conversation turned in this direction, Maliheh's mother would insist that none of the servants should be present in Khanom Jan's living room. She was afraid they'd go and report it and the State would come and "collect" all her antiques. She didn't seem to grasp that people like Uncle never do anything, the silly creatures only talk. As for the ones I know, if the State were to confiscate their honor they'd even reconcile themselves to this—so long as they eventually get their pensions!

I was telling you about the events of that day … When Uncle once gets into his critical mood, even wild horses can't stop him. By now he was saying to Mama, "Do you remember the winter of a couple of years back? What crashes, I tell you, what crashes! All the squares in the city frozen over, all the streets with big cracks. But you think it was a lesson for those in charge? Not on your life! I told the mayor, 'There is no point in renewing the asphalt every year, my dear sir: one must rethink the situation radically!' But what do we have? The same old mess again this year. At least there is reason to be thankful that this year the cold isn't as bad as it was then."

At this point I chipped in, "Didn't you say there was no precedent for this year's cold in the last twenty-five years?"

Ali Aqa started to laugh. Uncle retorted, "I was speaking about the amount of snow, madam." Then he turned to Ali Aqa, "Watch where you're going, my friend. Don't overtake! Don't overtake!"

You would have thought Ali Aqa was about to overtake another vehicle.

"Gently on the gas pedal, Ali Aqa!"

You would have thought he was pushing it all the way to the floor.

"Slow down! Low gear! Careful!"

Poor old Ali Aqa. I said, "Ali Aqa, what Uncle means is, 'Drive the way *he* drives when the sun is out and the roads are empty.'"

This time Ali Aqa swallowed his laugh. "See here, my lady," said Uncle Ardeshir, "I've been driving more years than you've been on earth."

Fortunately, I've gotten used to Uncle's way of putting me down, and it no longer gets to me.

I said, "O.K., so what? Take the case of Zahra. She's been cooking pilaf for forty years and she still gets a clobbering from Kadkhoda every day, because her rice is either practically raw or stinks of smoke. What you said doesn't prove a thing."

Mama didn't really notice what I had said and why I had said it. All she could think of was that one should feel sorry for Zahra. She mumbled, "Poor thing! Next time Kadkhoda comes to town, I must tell him that he should be ashamed, and should think of his own white beard and his wife's white hair."

I was about to say, "Kadkhoda no longer works for you to give him orders."

But Uncle, who had been upset by my previous remarks, didn't let me even open my mouth and went on: "Of course, in your opinion it doesn't prove a thing. The wise men of old used to say, 'Practice makes perfect.' Of course, by your standards they didn't know what they were talking about…"

I felt certain that the so-called Ancients had also said other things which would fit the case of both Uncle and Zahra. But rack my empty skull as I would, I couldn't think of anything—I was really fed up!

Ali Aqa was very glum too: I could tell by his expression. Whenever I fail to get the better of Uncle, Ali Aqa is upset. Uncle was thoroughly pleased with himself at having tweaked my nose: he lounged further back in the car and puffed away merrily at his pipe.

I said, "Uncle, can you get me a driver's license?" All I really had in mind was to find some sort of reply to him: the license itself wasn't important. Another little corner of my mind was vaguely preoccupied with Kadkhoda and Zahra, since the poor devils' situation was no longer as flourishing as it had been, though one would have thought they ought to be sitting pretty. I still couldn't think of a suitable retort to Uncle, and I was fit to be tied. The only thing I could think of was a saying like, "Education is wasted on the unqualified," but I knew that if I said this, it would backfire on me. So I said nothing.

Uncle Ardeshir now chose to answer my request: "No. When you reach the legal age, then maybe."

You'd think I wasn't bright enough. "But you said you know people. O.K., so ask them to test me, can't you? It's not just a question of my age."

I didn't dare suggest he should get my I.D. card altered and add two lousy years to my age. I had once mentioned this possibility some time before, and Mama had blown up. On that occasion, in an attempt to calm her down, Uncle had said, "Something like that is totally out of the question." Oh yeah? So far, Auntie Fakhri has had her I.D. card changed at least four times. Amir even says that she is now twelve years younger than her real age. So what do you mean, "It's out of the question?!" Once more Uncle declared, "Can't be done, my dear. The country has laws—and for good reason too."

All this lot are always on about illegalities—and I don't mean the things they say about the condition of the road surfaces. When the State seized the lands for reforestation, you should've heard how Uncle held forth. I told you about it, didn't I? He strode up and down, going into every detail: "What does this country need a forest for? It's *already* a jungle, yes sir! Even in the most backward of all countries, sir, a land title is recognized, but in this wilderness nothing commands any respect."

I came back at him on this: "You once said about the lands business there *is* no law. So how do we stand now …?"

At this point, Mama gave me a poke from behind and my words were cut off halfway. From Ali Aqa's sidelong glance I realized I had gone too far. Yet Uncle Ardeshir himself, in the early days when the seizure of the lands was first proclaimed, babbled and ranted and raved at such length that you would've thought he'd never leave it alone till his dying day.* Of course, even then, I was aware that all this huffing and puffing was mere empty talk and would never go beyond the four walls of the house, eventually dying away altogether after a few days. As I've told you, it's always the same, whatever disaster befalls them. It makes you mad! In fact, I get madder with people who meekly listen to bullying than I do with those who inflict it. You understand what I mean? I mean I get really mad with spineless people. And yet, at the same time, one has to listen to all their nonsense and watch their ineffectual behavior, while not breathing a word oneself.

I was expecting Uncle to chew me out for what I'd just said, but fortunately since he had gotten well into his stride talking about the merits of jurisprudence, he hadn't noticed anything at all. As a result, I felt at a loss, and myself paid no attention to what he was saying. You

---

* This refers to the Land Reform program from 1962 onwards, which formed part of Mohammad Reza Shah's White Revolution, and which naturally involved great resentment on the part of the big landowners.

might say that even on a bright day my ear was not well tuned in to Uncle's remarks, let alone when he was holding forth on a dark night! After all, as I've already said, the business of the driving license wasn't really important—my only concern was to come up with some sort of retort to Uncle. I was trying to find something to say besides my reference to "Education for the unqualified." Finally I got it: "Uncle, I believe the old-time philosophers also said another thing, namely, 'Brackish soil will not yield a harvest, sowing it is labor in vain.'"

Uncle no longer recalled what I was driving at, so he replied, "Ye-e-es. They did say that, and they said well. All right—so what's your point?"

For a moment I was about to say, "My point was: give me an N!"* But I was afraid he might instead give me some bread to chew on, and I wouldn't find the opportunity to say what I really had in mind. So I blurted out right away, "What I was thinking of was the link between Zahra's pilaf and your driving."

Mama cried out, "Oh God! Oh Lord! Deliver me from this girl! Why do you have to be so rude?"

Ali Aqa's face was wreathed in smiles. Uncle managed a heavy, meaningful "ye-e-es" and then clamped his teeth on the stem of his pipe.

I began to feel a bit better, especially when I remembered it was a holiday.

So much for that. I don't have that much to tell you about the reception at the house of Erfaq od-Dowleh's prospective son-in-law. However, as soon as we entered—no!, let me first tell you about the house itself. You can't imagine what a pretentious hodgepodge it all was. People were saying that two million *tomans* had been spent on it.

Spending two million *tomans*, even on all this tastelessness, demands real skill. Let's be fair. You couldn't help thinking you'd walked into the Adalat Furniture Emporium. There was a chandelier hanging from the middle of the ceiling of the salon which had one hundred and

---

* The reference is to a game (*mosha'ara*) in which each contestant tries to match a line of poetry given by another player. The matching is done by the rhyme-letter of one line and the initial letter of the next. In the present case, there is an additional twist inasmuch as the letter "N" in Persian rhymes with the collo-quial word for "bread," and Suri suspects that her uncle is bound to confuse the two.

fifty branches. You have to wonder, when it has one hundred and fifty branches, should it still be called a chandelier? I don't know. Anyway, every single one of the one hundred and fifty had been lit. And even that wasn't enough: the scoundrels had also lit all the wall sconces. I don't know why, but with all these furnishings from Adalat and the assembled crowd of all shapes and sizes, the room still seemed both bare and cold. All the time I was afraid that under this bright light everybody would see the wet patch on my pants. (Did I remember to tell you that before we set out, I had a fall in the snow?) My main concern was to sit down as soon as possible. There was an empty chair at the far end of the room, so I marked it down and headed straight for it. But by the time I got to the middle of the room—hey presto!—everybody sat down, just as though they were playing musical chairs. I was the only one left standing. Uncle Ardeshir and Mama both kept signaling me from afar, with eyes and eyebrows, to sit down. Did they think I didn't want to sit, for crying out loud? With my shabby blouse and my soaking-wet pants, standing in the middle of a crowd, especially under a one-hundred-and-fifty-branch chandelier, was certainly no fun. To make matters worse, everybody was staring at me like some sad little thing. It was as though I was supposed to indicate "friend or foe" in some stupid game. I was practically dying with embarrassment. I placed my hand over the wet patch on my pants, and feeling utterly dizzy and dumbstruck I did a 360-degree turn until I found an empty chair once more. I dashed at it like a bullet. For a moment, I nearly overturned a glass-top table holding fine crystal goblets. Then I crashed into a waiter who was entering just that moment, carrying a tea-tray. However, both encounters passed off without mishap, and I eventually managed to secure my chair and sat down.

But, right to the end of the party, I never properly got my breath back, especially as—casting my eye around—I noticed that I had taken my place at the wrong end, that is to say with the groom's family. I didn't know a soul.

At first, nobody said a word, but when they did begin to speak, they all started at once. I neither heard nor understood a single thing. All their remarks whirled around in my head in utter confusion.

One seemed to be saying, "Anyone he'd wanted, he could've had, a groom like that ...." Another one at the other end was saying, "Breeding and good background ... the long line of Erfaq od-Dowleh's family ... such things can't simply be bought ..."

I was still immersed in my contemplation of the scene around me. On my right three elderly men were seated on a sofa, and I really couldn't understand how they were related to the groom. The one farthest away from me spoke in a very precise manner, and when he did so, he sprayed his spit in all directions and hissed his S's. All this made his remarks seem particularly comical. The old fellow in the middle appeared to be deaf, because he made his hand into a speaking trumpet and placed it around his ear, then pointing his ear in the direction from which he guessed the voice was coming. Furthermore, I think he must've been hearing everything wrong, since the person speaking would raise his voice to say, "No, sir! You aren't following me." This was followed by more hissing and spitting. The third old guy neither spoke nor listened, but kept on swallowing baklava. At the same time he would look at people from under his bushy brows, in such a way that he might have been watching you from under water. Furthermore, his eyes were open wide, and their lids were both heavy and abnormally red.

On my left was sitting a plump lady, hung from head to foot with earrings, necklaces and bangles. As soon as I looked at her, she jumped up, kissed me all over the face, and said, "God bless my soul! You're Parvaneh's sister, aren't you, dearie?"

"No! Parvaneh hasn't got a sister."

The lady seemed really upset that I wasn't Parvaneh's sister, and that she didn't have a sister anyway. She asked again, "You're sure she doesn't? So she only has one brother."

I replied, "No. Two."

It was as though having two brothers made up for Parvaneh's not having a sister. Delighted, she said, "Uh huh! Which ones are they?"

"They're both in America."

She eyed me narrowly: "Dear Farhang, the brother of dear Hushang, is in Germany too, you know."

After that, till the party was over, she paid me no further attention. So much the better, since I simply don't know how to talk to strangers...

Everybody was sitting down, but for some reason whenever I looked at them, it seemed as if they were all fidgeting around. The sound of their voices was like the hubbub at the beginning of class before the teacher comes in. Once in a while, however, Uncle's voice rose above the din. On one occasion he appeared to be saying to the groom, "I have had the pleasure of meeting your parents, but not your younger sibling. Where does he reside these days?"

I had the impression that the poor fellow had not understood the word "sibling," because Uncle now phrased it, "your younger brother." The groom's reply was lost in the uproar, so I never got what he said. But I did hear Uncle's voice once more. He now appeared to be talking to Erfaq od-Dowleh about such topics as memories of the past, the herb-gardener of Amin od-Dowleh, Lokhti Avenue* and similar things. When people like Uncle speak of these bygone times in Tehran, it strikes me as an interesting sort of place. I dearly wish that the city gates and the moat and so on were still there. It would be nice too if the streets still retained their former names—don't you agree? There is a map of Tehran in our house: perhaps you've seen it? It used to belong to Grandad. It's *very* interesting. When you look at it, you imagine it's of an entirely different place: not just because the Tehran of today has grown so huge, but because the place names have all been changed. Surely that's why Tehran is now so utterly without roots—you understand what I'm trying to say? Let me put it like this: as soon as it gets a bit of history, they start to modernize it again, changing its appearance and all its various names.

But let's move on now. I was getting thoroughly fed up with this party. They kept on dishing out food. When you've got nothing to do, you're supposed to stuff your face. I myself ate a ton of roasted melonseeds. I avoided looking at Mama in case she was biting her lip in disapproval. There was so much food laid out on the dining table that it made you lose your appetite. I mentioned this to Mama who said, "Not at all! It's the melonseeds that've spoilt your appetite."

Uncle now joined us and turned to Mama. "No, Amir was obviously talking nonsense. In the first place that fellow is older, and secondly he has a German wife."

I expected Mama to understand his remark no better than I did. But it seemed that she did understand because she eyed the whole gathering narrowly, and after loading some carrots onto my plate, she said to Uncle, "That Amir guy will make you a hundred knives, but not a single one has a handle."

---

* Lokhti Avenue = literally, "Bareness Avenue." Different explanations are given for this name: Jamalzadeh's *Farhang-e Loghat-e 'Amiyaneh* (Dictionary of Common Expressions), Tehran, 1338-41/1959-62 says it was an old name for Sa'di Avenue in recognition of its once having no buildings. Another version (as supplied by Professor H. Farmayan) explains it as "Robbers' Avenue," the street where people were stripped naked in muggings.

I couldn't help asking, "What's that you say, Mama? What did Amir do?"

"Nothing, my dear," Uncle cut in. "If you're feeling tired, we'll leave immediately after supper."

I burst out, "Oh, that's great!" Uncle now gave me a real dirty look, so I hastened to say, "Yes, yes. Of course. It would be preferable!"—and I even made my voice sound like Uncle's.

He gave a little laugh. I've no idea why he wanted to be kind for once. Perhaps he felt sorry that I'd had such a bad time at the party.

On the way back I expected that everybody would be talking about the new family connections that had been established, but no one said a thing. All the talk was about the downed telephone lines once more and similar such stuff. When Uncle Ardeshir got to his favorite phrase, "Nobody gives a damn, sir ... ," I fell asleep.

Did I forget to tell you? The groom was very much like ourselves. What I mean is, he was a very ordinary sort of guy. His whole appearance was just average. Maybe Parvaneh doesn't even love him. I've no idea.